Slaves and Captains

Rhodri Jones

A version of *Benito Cereno* by Herman Melville

ANDRE DEUTSCH

First published in 1988 by
André Deutsch Limited
105–106 Great Russell Street, London WC1B 3LJ

British Library Cataloguing in Publication Data

Jones, Rhodri
    Slaves and captains.
    I. Title
    823'.914 [F]

    ISBN 0 233 98356 2

Phototypeset by AKM Associates (UK) Ltd
Ajmal House, Hayes Road, Southall, London
Printed in Great Britain by
WBC Limited, Bristol and Maesteg

Slaves and Captains

Contents

Foreword *vii*

1   The Strange Ship *1*

2   On Board *7*

3   The Misfortunes of the *San Dominick* *15*

4   The Chained African *21*

5   Suspicions Grow *29*

6   Various Encounters *41*

7   The Boat Arrives *51*

8   The Shave *58*

9   Lunch in the Cabin *69*

10   The Breeze *75*

11   A Flash of Revelation *81*

12   The Fight for the *San Dominick* *88*

13   Don Benito's Statement *94*

14   The End of the Story *113*

Afterword *117*

Foreword

Have you heard of Herman Melville, the nineteenth-century American writer? Even if you don't know his name, you have probably heard of 'Moby Dick', the white whale in Herman Melville's novel of that title which the half-crazed Captain Ahab is obsessed with and determined to hunt down.

Most people have heard of Moby Dick though few have read the novel. I regret to say that I have never been able to get through it myself, though I have tried twice. The long digressions on the natural history of the whale and Melville's long-winded meandering style have defeated me.

So when I recently came across Melville's story *Benito Cereno* and started to read it, I didn't hold out much hope. You can imagine my surprise, therefore, when I found myself totally gripped by it and compelled to go on reading to find out what happened next. It was like being caught in a web because it wasn't quite clear what was going on, and I was drawn into the events to try to find out the truth.

Everything is seen through the eyes of the American, Captain Delano, but as I read there was a suspicion that things were not exactly as they seemed. Odd events happened, and although the captain managed to explain them away to his own satisfaction, the reader — or this reader at least — felt uneasy. Was Captain Delano right? Or was there something strange going on?

And then there was the attitude of Captain Delano himself. There was something smug and complacent about him. He was generous towards the black people on board the ship and thought of himself as a liberal-minded person, but his views are not those of a liberal person today, and there was something disquieting about them.

Finally, when the true nature of what had happened is revealed, it came like a thunderbolt. The scales drop from Captain Delano's eyes, and from the reader's as well. The brutality that is uncovered is horrifying, and the real reason why Captain Delano was taken in is made clear.

So reading Melville's story was for me an enthralling experience. But there was still more to discover. Melville based his story on real events. What Melville described actually happened to an American captain and was recorded by him. When I read the original source, it was clear how closely Melville had followed it. I was astounded. *Benito Cereno* was not just a story, it was a kind of historical document too.

I wanted to share with others the excitement I felt on reading the story and discovering its factual origins. But there remained the problem of Melville's prose style which many readers would find difficult and off-putting. So what I have done is to present Melville's ideas and the facts from the original source in a simplified form. I hope this will not weaken the story's power. I hope you will find the events described as strange and horrifying and thought-provoking as I did.

It is worth making one further point. Melville referred to the slaves as 'the blacks' and as 'Negroes'. Nowadays, we would talk about 'black people' and would not use the word 'Negroes'. However, I have retained these expressions in that part of the story taken from the official documents of the trial which were written at the time of the events.

Chapter 1
The Strange Ship

Not long after dawn on the eighteenth of August 1799, Captain Amasa Delano was awakened in his berth by his chief mate.

'I think you should know, sir,' the mate said. 'There is a strange ship coming into the bay.'

Captain Delano roused himself and reached for his clothes. The day before, he had anchored his ship, the *Bachelor's Delight*, in the harbour of St Maria, a small uninhabited island towards the southern end of the long coast of Chile. Captain Delano was from Duxbury in Massachusetts. His ship was engaged in hunting seals and in general trade in the area and had a valuable cargo on board. He had touched at St Maria to take on water.

As he dressed, Captain Delano thought about the mate's report. It was rare to encounter another ship in those waters. He hurried on deck.

It was one of those mornings peculiar to that coast. Everything was silent and still. Everything was grey. The sea, though undulating with currents, seemed fixed. It had a surface smoothness like waved lead that has cooled and set in the smelter's mould. The sky was like a grey overcoat. Flights of restless grey birds skimmed low and fitfully over the face of the sea as swallows do over meadows before storms. They seemed part of the restless grey mists that flitted across sky and sea. They were like shadows fore-shadowing deeper shadows to come.

'She shows no colours,' the mate pointed out.

Captain Delano was surprised. He took the telescope from the mate and focused it on the mysterious vessel. What the mate said was true. It was certainly unusual. It was the custom among peaceful seamen of all nations to hoist their flag on entering any harbour, even in an uninhabited area like this, if there was any chance of another ship being berthed there.

'D'you think she's a freebooter?' the mate asked uneasily.

Captain Delano considered for a moment. This was a lonely and lawless coast. There were many stories of piracy and danger. Captain Delano's surprise could have deepened into suspicion, but he had a very trusting nature. He found it difficult to think evil of his fellow man unless there was the most definite and undeniable proof. No one could doubt that he had a kind heart, but only the wise may tell whether his view of human nature showed more than ordinary perception — given what humanity is capable of. Whatever the case, he saw no reason to be alarmed by the ship's lack of colours and jump to the conclusion that she intended to make trouble.

'I think not,' he said.

He continued to examine the ship through his telescope. If there had been any misgivings on first observing the strange vessel, they were soon dismissed. Any seaman would have felt the same. Because the ship was in danger. In navigating into the harbour, it was drawing too close to land. There was a sunken reef off its bow. From this it appeared that the ship was not only a stranger to Captain Delano but also to these waters. Therefore, it couldn't possibly be a freebooter.

With great interest, Captain Delano watched the man-oeuvrings of the ship. His vision was hampered by the wispy cloud that clung to the hull. Through these vapours, the morning light from her cabin streamed strongly enough like a kind of sun. Surrounded as it was by the creeping mists, it looked like the sinister eye of one of those mysterious Indian women you see in the evening in the Plaza in Lima, peering through the loop-hole of her shawl. The sun itself, now a hemisphere on the rim of the horizon, looked as though it was being drawn along by the strange ship as it approached the harbour.

It could just have been the mists playing tricks, but the longer Captain Delano watched, the more puzzled he became by the manoeuvres of the ship. It was difficult to make out whether she intended to enter the harbour or not. It was a complete mystery what the ship was up to. The apparent uncertainty of her movements was increased by the wind. It had breezed up a little during the night, and now it was light and making progress difficult.

'What is she doing?' the mate asked with some exasperation.

'Perhaps she's in distress,' Captain Delano suggested. He ordered the whale-boat to be dropped.

'Take care,' the mate warned. 'I don't trust her.'

'No, no,' returned the captain. 'There's no danger. At least we can help to pilot her in.'

The night before, a fishing-party of seamen had gone some distance to a rocky area out of sight of the *Bachelor's Delight* and had returned an hour or two before daybreak with a good catch of fish. Captain Delano, presuming that the strange ship might have long been out of touch with land, had several baskets of the fish put into the boat and pulled away.

He urged his men to make haste. The vessel was still too near the sunken reef. They had to warn her of the danger. But before they could get close to the ship, the wind shifted, and even though it was light, began to head the vessel off.

The wind also partly broke up the mists that drifted about her, and the ship became more clearly visible. Rising out of the lead-coloured waves, with shreds of fog raggedly furring her here and there, she looked like a whitewashed monastery after a thunderstorm — one of those you see perched on a dark cliff in the Pyrenees.

And it wasn't just a fanciful imagination that made the captain think for a moment that this was a ship-load of monks before him. There really did seem to be in the hazy distance throngs of dark-hooded heads peering over the bulwarks. And now and then through the open port-holes other dark moving figures could dimly be made out, like Black Friars pacing the cloisters.

But as the whale-boat drew nearer to the ship, these impressions were modified. The true nature of the vessel became clear. It was a Spanish merchantman of the first class, carrying African slaves, together with other valuable freight, from one colonial port to another.

It was very large and had once been a very fine vessel. Others like it were to be encountered in those waters in those days — vessels which had once been Acapulco treasure-ships, or frigates sold off from the Spanish king's navy. They still showed signs of their former glory, though now reduced in the world, like Italian palaces which had been neglected and allowed to run down.

Closer to, the reason for the strange white appearance of the ship was revealed. It was the result of slovenly lack of care. The spars, ropes and great parts of the bulwarks looked woolly and had clearly not seen scraper, tar and brush for a long time. The keel and the framework of ribs rising out of it might have come from Ezekiel's Valley of Dry Bones.

No structural alteration had been made to the ship. It looked just as it had done when it was a warship — except that there were no guns to be seen.

The tops were large. They were railed about with what had once been octagonal net-work, but this was now in a sad state of disrepair. They hung over the ship like three ruinous aviaries. Indeed, in one of them, perched on a ratline, was a white noddy, a strange bird so called because of its character

— they were so dozy and lazy you could often catch them by hand at sea.

The castellated forecastle was battered and mouldy. It looked like some ancient turret which had been assaulted and captured long ago and left to decay. Towards the stern, there were two high-raised quarter-galleries which opened out from the unoccupied state-cabin whose dead-lights were hermetically closed and caulked in spite of the mild weather. The balustrades of the galleries were covered here and there with dry tindery sea-moss, and the balconies hung over the sea as if it were the Grand Canal in Venice.

But the main relic of grandeur was the large shield-like stern-piece. Oval in shape, it was intricately carved with the arms of Castile and Leon, surrounded by mythological figures and symbolic devices. The one above the arms showed a dark satyr in a mask holding his foot on the prostrate neck of a writhing figure which was also masked.

It was difficult to make out whether the ship had a figure-head or only a plain beak because of the canvas which was wrapped around that part. It could have been to protect it while it was undergoing refurbishment, or else out of a sense of decency to hide its decay.

Below the canvas was a kind of pedestal, and along the forward side of this someone — a sailor playing a joke perhaps — had roughly painted or chalked some words. They were in Spanish and read 'Sequid vuestro jefe', that is, 'Follow your leader'. On the tarnished headboards nearby, stately capitals, once gilt, announced the ship's name, SAN DOMINICK. Tricklings of copper-spike rust streaked and corroded each letter. Dark festoons of sea-grass slimily swept to and fro over the name like mourning weeds with every hearse-like roll of the hull.

At last, the whale-boat came alongside. The men hooked it from the bow towards the gangway amidships. Its keel, while yet some inches separated from the hull, harshly grated as though against a sunken coral reef.

'It's barnacles, captain,' cried one of the men.

It was true. A huge bunch of congealed barnacles clung onto the side below the waterline like a wart. It seemed clear that the ship had suffered from long calms and baffling winds somewhere in those seas.

Chapter 2
On Board

Captain Delano climbed the side and reached the deck. He was immediately surrounded by a noisy mob of Africans and Spaniards. There were more black men than white, which was unusual, except that this was clearly a slave transportation-ship.

Africans and Spaniards together poured out in one language and in one voice a common tale of suffering. The slave women, of whom there were many, were loudest in their lamentations. Scurvy and fever had swept off many, especially among the Spaniards. Off Cape Horn they had narrowly escaped shipwreck. Then for days together they had lain becalmed without a wind. Their provisions were low. They had next to no water. Their lips at that very moment were dry and parched.

While eager tongues bombarded him with their story, Captain Delano took in their tales and the scene around him.

Boarding a large and populous ship, especially a foreign one with an anonymous crew such as Lascars or Manilla men, is in many ways similar to entering a strange house with strange inhabitants in a strange land. Both conceal their interiors till the last moment, the house by its walls and blinds, the ship by its high bulwarks like ramparts. But there is this difference. When the living spectacle that the ship contains is suddenly and completely revealed, it has a sense of enchantment, especially when contrasted with the blank ocean that surrounds it. The ship seems unreal. The strange costumes, gestures and faces are like some shadowy mirage which has emerged from the sea and which could immediately be swallowed up again.

It may have been some sensation such as this which heightened the scene in Captain Delano's mind. What particularly struck him were the figures of four elderly grey-haired Africans. With their heads like lopped-off willow tops, they stood out from the others. They were crouched, sphynx-like, in contrast to the tumult below them, one on the starboard cat-head, another on the larboard, and the remaining pair face to face on the opposite bulwarks above the main-chains.

They each had bits of unstranded old rope in their hands which they were unpicking into oakum, a small heap of which lay by their sides. They worked with a sort of stoical self-content, and accompanied the task with a continuous low monotonous chant — droning and drooling away like grey-headed bagpipers playing a funeral march.

The quarter-deck rose into an ample elevated poop. On the forward edge of this a row of six other Africans sat cross-legged at regular intervals, raised like the oakum-pickers some eight feet above the general throng. Each of them had a rusty hatchet in his hand which he was engaged in scouring like a kitchen scullion with a bit of brick and a rag. Alongside them were small stacks of hatchets, their rusted edges turned forward waiting to be sharpened.

The four oakum-pickers would occasionally speak to people in the crowd below, but the six hatchet-polishers spoke to no one. Neither did they breathe a whisper among themselves. They sat concentrating on their work, except when two by two they clashed their hatchets together every now and then like cymbals, making a barbarous din. How typical, Captain Delano thought, of the way black men love to combine work with entertainment. All six, unlike most of those on deck, had the uncouth appearance of men who had come straight from Africa.

The captain took in these ten figures with scores that were less conspicuous in one quick comprehensive glance. The hubbub of voices around him continued, but he grew impatient with it. He searched about to find who was in command of the ship.

The Spanish captain was leaning against the main-mast. He was gentlemanly and reserved-looking, rather younger than one would expect. His clothes were exceedingly rich, but his face showed signs of sleepless nights and recent worries. He stood passively by, alternately casting a dreary spiritless look on his excited people and then an unhappy glance towards his visitor. It was as though he were prepared to let his suffering people plead their own misery, or else he despaired of being able to restrain them for the moment.

By his side stood a black man of small stature. Every now and then, this man would turn his peasant face up to look at his master with an expression in which sorrow and affection were mixed, just as a shepherd's dog would do.

Struggling through the throng, Captain Delano advanced on the Spaniard. 'My dear sir,' he assured him, 'you have all my sympathy. I shall give you all the assistance that lies in my power.'

The Spaniard introduced himself as Don Benito Cereno. He was courteous but remote. This Captain Delano put down to the formality typical of people of his nation and to the dark shadow of ill-health that hung over him.

But there was no time to waste in mere compliments. Captain Delano returned to the gangway and ordered the basket of fish to be brought up. The wind still continued light so it would be some hours before the ship could be brought into harbour. The whale-boat was sent back to the *Bachelor's Delight* to fetch as much water as it would carry, together with whatever soft bread the steward might have, all the remaining pumpkins on board, a box of sugar, and a dozen of the captain's private bottles of cider.

Not many minutes after the boat had pushed off, the wind died away entirely. The tide turned, and the Spanish ship began to drift helplessly back out to sea. The people on deck grew agitated.

'Don't worry,' Captain Delano reassured them. 'It won't last long. Be of good cheer.'

He spoke in Spanish and congratulated himself on his command of the language which he had picked up during his frequent voyages along the Spanish Main. It was good to be able to comfort these people in their own tongue.

Captain Delano was now alone with them on deck and had the opportunity to build on his first impressions. He was filled with pity for Spaniards and Africans alike and the suffering that showed in their faces from lack of water and provisions. This long-continued suffering seemed to have brought out the less pleasing qualities of the Africans while at the same time reducing the authority of the Spanish captain over them. But in circumstances like these, that was only to be expected. Everywhere — in armies, navies, cities, even families — in nature herself — nothing undermines good order and discipline more than misery.

Still, Captain Delano reflected, if Don Benito had been a man of greater energy, he could have kept a firmer hold on the situation. But the Spaniard's physical and mental weakness — either part of his nature or brought on by recent hardship — was only too apparent.

He seemed to be in a permanent state of depression. It was as if having been so long mocked with hope he could not believe that rescue had arrived. That day, or by evening at the latest, his ship would be lying at anchor. He would have plenty of water for his people and a fellow captain to advise and befriend him. Yet none of this seemed to cheer him in any way. His mind appeared to be confused, if not still more seriously affected. Being shut up in these oak walls, chained to one dull round of command, unable to deal with the disorder around him — all of these had taken their toll. He reminded Captain Delano of a hypochondriac abbot as he moved slowly about, at times suddenly pausing, starting or staring, biting his lip, biting his finger-nail, flushing, growing pale, twitching his beard, together with other signs of an absent or moody mind.

As previously suggested, his body was as out of condition as his spirit. He was rather tall, but seemed never to have been full-bodied. Now, with nervous worry, he was almost worn to a skeleton. He seemed to be suffering from some kind of chest complaint. His voice was like that of someone with only half a lung. When he spoke, it was in a kind of husky whisper.

It wasn't surprising that his servant followed him apprehensively as he tottered about in this state. Sometimes the man gave his master his arm or took his handkerchief out of his pocket for him. He performed these duties with an affectionate eagerness that was more like that of a son or a brother than a menial. It was this kind of service, Captain Delano reflected, that had gained for Africans the reputation of being the most pleasant body-servants in the world. There was no need for their masters to be on stiffly superior terms with them. They could treat them with informality and trust, less like servants than like devoted companions.

It gave Captain Delano warm satisfaction to see how well the servant conducted himself, especially when compared with the noisy wildness of the Africans in general and the sullen slovenly attitude of the Spaniards.

But even the attentions of the servant, whose name was Babo, seemed to have no effect in rousing the half-mad Don Benito from his gloomy inertia. Not that that was precisely the way Captain Delano saw the Spaniard. For the present, he regarded Don Benito's personal state of mind simply as a symptom of the ship's general malaise.

Even so, Captain Delano couldn't help feeling somewhat concerned by what he took at the time to be Don Benito's unfriendly indifference towards himself. The Spaniard's manner conveyed a sort of sour and gloomy disdain which he seemed to make no attempt to disguise. But out of charity, Captain Delano put this down to the effect sickness had on people. He could remember previous instances where prolonged physical suffering on a certain type of person had resulted in all social instincts of kindness being forgotten. It was as if, forced to eat black bread themselves, they thought it only right that everyone who came near them should do the same.

But then, even though Captain Delano had been sympathetic in judging the Spaniard from the beginning, he wondered if he had been sympathetic enough. What basically displeased him was Don Benito's reserve. But this same reserve was shown towards all but his faithful personal attendant. Even when formal reports were made to him at stated times according to standard sea-usage by underlings, either white, mulatto or black, Don Benito could scarcely listen to them without betraying contempt or distaste. His manner on such occasions must have been like that of his fellow countryman, Emperor Charles V, just before his retirement from the throne when his thoughts were aleady on the monastery he was to go to.

This petulant dislike of his position was indicated in almost everything connected with it. Proud and moody, he did not condescend to give orders himself. When orders were necessary, they were relayed to his body-servant. He in turn conveyed them to runners, alert Spanish boys or slave boys, like pages or pilot-fish hovering round Don Benito continually within easy call, who transferred them to their ultimate destination. Seeing this withdrawn invalid gliding about, silent and totally lacking in interest, no landsman could have dreamed that this man, while at sea, held power against which there was no earthly appeal.

It had to be assumed that the Spaniard was the helpless victim of mental disorder. Unless his lack of involvement was to some degree deliberate. All commanders of large ships adopt, to a greater or less extent, a manner which conceals any show of their power and their humanity. The man is transformed into a block, or rather into a loaded cannon which has nothing to say until there is an emergency, a call for thunder. If this was the icy yet conscientious policy Don Benito was pursuing, he was taking it to an unhealthy extreme.

Such an approach might have been harmless or even appropriate in a well-appointed vessel, such as the *San Dominick* when she set off on her voyage. But given the present condition of the ship, it was perverse of the Spaniard to persist in his attitude which could only be the result of hard self-restraint. Perhaps the Spaniard thought that captains should behave the same way as gods. They should show no emotion at any time.

But more likely, this appearance of lack of interest was merely an attempt on the part of the Spaniard to disguise from others the mental weakness that was becoming more apparent to himself. It wasn't some deep-seated plan, just a feeble effort to conceal the truth. In any case, whether Don Benito's manner was designed or not, it was the same to everyone. Captain Delano began to feel more easy. At least Don Benito's reserve was not being directed personally at him.

Captain Delano's thoughts were not solely taken up by the Spaniard. The noisy confusion of the suffering inhabitants of the *San Dominick* repeatedly forced itself on him. It was made all the more striking by the contrast it presented with the quiet orderliness of his own ship and her comfortable family of a crew. There were obvious breaches not just of discipline but of decency. This could only be put down to the absence of those subordinate deck-officers who, along with other duties, normally act as the policing force on a crowded ship. It was true that the old oakum-pickers appeared at times to be trying to keep order among their countrymen, but although they succeeded now and then in quelling trifling disputes between one man and another, they could do little or nothing towards establishing general quiet.

The *San Dominick* was like a transatlantic emigrant ship. No doubt in such a ship there are some individuals among its living freight who are no more trouble than crates or bales. But when these try to calm their rougher companions, they are likely to be less effective than the unfriendly arm of the mate. What the *San Dominick* needed was what emigrant ships have — stern superior officers. But on these decks not so much as a fourth mate was to be seen.

Chapter 3
The Misfortunes of the
San Dominick

Captain Delano was curious to know more of the misfortunes that had brought this about. He had learned something of the voyage from the wails that had greeted him when he first boarded the ship, yet he had gained no clear impression of the details. Without doubt, the best account would be given by the captain. To begin with, he was reluctant to ask him for fear of provoking a cold rebuff. But eventually he plucked up courage and approached Don Benito.

'I am most concerned about your situation,' he said. 'Please tell me more about the ship's misfortunes. I might then be in a better position to help you. I should be most obliged if you would tell me what happened.'

Don Benito faltered. Then like a sleepwalker who has been disturbed, he stared vacantly at Captain Delano and ended by looking down at the deck. He stayed like this so long that Captain Delano was almost equally disconcerted and unintentionally almost as rude. He turned suddenly from Don Benito and walked forward to one of the Spanish seamen to get the information he wanted. But he had hardly gone five paces when Don Benito called out to him.

'Please come back. I am so sorry. My mind must have

become a blank. I am only too ready to tell you.'

While Don Benito related his story, the two captains stood on the after part of the main-deck. This was a private place. No one else was near except Don Benito's servant, Babo.

The Spaniard began in his husky whisper. 'We sailed from Buenos Ayres, a hundred and ninety days ago bound for Lima. We had a full complement of officers and men, with several cabin-passengers — some fifty Spaniards in all. We had a general cargo — hardware, Paraguay tea and the like — and' (he pointed forward) 'that parcel of Negroes. There were over three hundred of them, but now there are not more than a hundred and fifty. Off Cape Horn we had heavy gales. In one incident at night we lost three of my best officers and fifteen sailors with the main-yard. The spar snapped under them in the slings as they tried to beat down the icy sail with heavers. To lighten the hull, the heavier sacks of cargo were thrown into the sea, as well as most of the water-pipes that were lashed on deck at the time. That was what eventually brought about the main cause of our suffering — that and the prolonged calms that occurred later. When —'

Here Don Benito was suddenly attacked by a fit of coughing that left him faint. It was brought on, no doubt, by his mental distress. His servant gave him his support. He drew a cordial from his pocket and placed it to his master's lips. Don Benito revived a little. The black man's arm still encircled his master, unwilling to let go until he had fully recovered. At the same time, the servant kept his eyes fixed on his master's face, as if to watch for the first sign of restored strength or relapse, whichever it might be.

The Spaniard went on, but his speech was broken and slurred like that of someone in a dream.

'Oh, my God! I would joyfully welcome the most terrible gales than have to live through what happened once more. But —'

His cough returned with increased violence. When this had subsided, he fell heavily against his supporter with reddened lips and closed eyes.

'His mind wanders,' Babo sighed plaintively. 'He was thinking of the plague that followed the gales. My poor poor master!'

He squeezed the fingers of one hand together in distress while with the other he wiped the Spaniard's mouth. He turned again to Captain Delano. 'Just be patient, Señor. These fits do not last long. Master will soon be himself.'

When Don Benito had revived, he continued. But his delivery was very broken. The substance of his story was this.

It appeared that after the ship had been tossed for many days in storms off the Cape, scurvy broke out and carried off numbers of both Spaniards and Africans. Eventually, they worked their way round into the Pacific. But their spars and sails were much damaged, and the surviving mariners, most of whom were ill, had difficulty in handling them. They were unable to lay a northerly course by the wind which was powerful. The result was that the ship was unmanageable. For successive days and nights she was blown north-westward. Then the breeze suddenly deserted her and she was becalmed in unknown waters.

The absence of the water-pipes now proved fatal to life, just as earlier their presence had menaced it. A malignant fever followed the scurvy, brought about by the shortage of water, or at least made worse by it. Together with the excessive heat during their prolonged calm, the fever made short work of it as it swept away whole families of the Africans and even more proportionally of the Spaniards.

As bad luck would have it, these included every remaining officer on board. Consequently they were unable to cope when south-west winds eventually followed the calm. The torn sails could only be dropped not furled when required and had gradually been reduced to the beggars' rags they now were.

At the earliest opportunity, Don Benito had made for Valdivia, the southernmost civilized port of Chile and

South America. There he hoped to procure replacements for the sailors that had been lost as well as supplies of water and sails. But nearing the coast, the cloudy weather had prevented him from even sighting the harbour.

Since then, the *San Dominick* had been tossed about by contrary winds like a shuttlecock, misled by currents, or grown weedy in calms. She was almost without a crew, almost without canvas, and almost without water. At intervals, more dead were given to the sea. Like a man lost in woods, the ship had more than once doubled back on her own track.

Painfully turning in the half embrace of his servant, Don Benito continued, 'But throughout these calamities I have to thank these Negroes you see. To your inexperienced eyes they may appear unruly. But they have conducted themselves with a greater sense of responsibility than even their owner could have thought possible in the circumstances.'

Here he fell heavily back again. Once more, his mind wandered. Then he recovered and went on less obscurely.

'Yes, their owner was quite right in assuring me that no fetters would be needed with them. They have always remained on deck as is usual in this kind of transportation — not thrust below as on the slave-ships. But they have also been freely permitted from the beginning to wander about within certain bounds at their pleasure.'

Again, the faintness returned. His mind rambled. But when he recovered, he resumed.

'But it is Babo here to whom, before God, I owe so much. To him I owe my own life. He too is the one who calmed his more ignorant brothers when they have from time to time grown restless.'

Babo bowed his face. 'Ah, master,' he sighed. 'Don't speak of me. Babo is nothing. What Babo has done was but duty.'

Captain Delano was full of admiration. 'Don Benito,' he cried, 'I envy you such a friend. I cannot call him a slave.'

As master and man stood before him, the black supporting

the white, Captain Delano could not help feeling how beautiful the relationship was. On one hand was faithfulness, and on the other trust. The scene was heightened by the contrast in dress, denoting their relative positions. The Spaniard wore a loose Chile jacket of dark velvet and white knee-breeches and stockings with silver buckles at the knee and instep. On his head he had a high-crowned sombrero made of fine straw. A slender silver-mounted sword hung from a knot in his sash. This was almost invariably part of a South American gentleman's dress at that time and even later, and it was for use as much as for decoration.

Occasionally, a nervous contortion of his body brought about some disarray in Don Benito's dress. But generally he presented an appearance of neatness in his attire which was in marked contrast to the unsightly disorder about him, especially in that squalid area forward of the main-mast which was wholly occupied by the Africans.

The servant wore nothing but wide trousers. Judging from their coarseness and patches, they were made out of some kind of topsail. They were clean and tied round the waist by a bit of unstranded rope. This, together with the subdued pleading air he had at times, made him look something like one of those begging friars of the Order of St Francis.

Blunt-thinking Captain Delano couldn't help feeling that Don Benito's clothes were not quite suitable for the time and place. It was strange too how they had survived with such elegance in the midst of his afflictions.

But there was nothing unusual about Don Benito's style of dress. He wore what most South Americans of his class wore. Though on the present voyage he had set out from Buenos Ayres, he had said that he himself was a native and resident of Chile. The inhabitants of Chile were somewhat behind the fashion of the day and had not taken to the plain coat and full-length trousers. Instead, they retained their provincial costume with some modifications, which was as picturesque as any in the world.

Even so, considering what had happened on the voyage and the paleness of Don Benito's face, his apparel was not what you would have expected. It made him look like an invalid courtier tottering about the streets of London at the time of the Plague.

The part of Don Benito's story that most interested Captain Delano was his account of the long calms and the way the ship had drifted about for so long. This was surprising considering the latitudes in question. He didn't say so, of course, but he couldn't help putting these delays down to clumsy seamanship and faulty navigation. It was easy to assume from Don Benito's small sallow hands that the young captain had got his command through the cabin-window not the hawse-hold. And indeed, if that were the case, why wonder at incompetence where youth, sickness and gentility were combined?

But compassion overwhelmed and drowned thoughts of criticism. Captain Delano again expressed his sympathy. Having now heard the whole story, he repeated his promise to see that Don Benito and his people were supplied with their immediate physical needs. And he went further. He would ensure that the ship had a large permanent supply of water as well as some sails and rigging. He was even prepared to spare three of his best seamen to act as temporary deck officers, though this would place himself in some difficulty.

With this help, the ship would be able to reach Conception without delay. There she could be refitted before proceeding to Lima, her destination.

This generous offer was bound to have an effect, even on an invalid. Don Benito's face lit up. Eager and agitated, he stared into Captain Delano's honest face. He seemed overcome with gratitude.

'This excitement is bad for master,' whispered the servant. He took Don Benito by the arm and with soothing words gently drew him aside.

Chapter 4
The Chained African

When Don Benito returned, Captain Delano was pained to observe that all his hope had been extinguished. It had been as short-lived and feverish as the colour in his cheeks.

After a while, Don Benito with a weary face looked up towards the poop. He invited Captain Delano to accompany him there to get the benefit of what little breath of wind might be stirring.

In order to reach this raised area, they had to go up a ladder on the last step of which on either side sat two of the hatchet-polishers like armorial supporters and sentries. Several times while listening to Don Benito's story, Captain Delano had started as the hatchet-polishers clashed their hatchets together. It seemed to him strange that such a disturbance should be allowed, especially in that part of the ship, and so close to a man who was ill. The hatchets looked anything but attractive, and their handlers were even less so. It was with some reluctance therefore, even a sense of shrinking, that Captain Delano agreed to Don Benito's suggestion, though he tried not to show it.

He could hardly refuse, especially as Don Benito solemnly insisted, bowing in the Spanish manner, that his guest should precede him up the ladder. This excessive show of politeness only served to make the deathly pallor of the Spaniard all the more distressing.

But it was with some hesitation that Captain Delano climbed the ladder between the hatchet-polishers. It was like running the gauntlet. As he stepped past them, he felt an apprehensive twinge in the calves of his legs.

Reaching the poop, he turned round. The whole file of hatchet-polishers, like so many organ-grinders, was still stupidly intent on their work. They seemed quite unaware of anything around them. Captain Delano laughed at himself. How could he have allowed that moment of nervous panic?

Shortly afterwards, standing with Don Benito looking foward upon the decks below, Captain Delano was disturbed by something he saw. It was like previous examples of lack of discipline he had noticed. Three African boys were sitting with two Spanish boys on the hatches. They were scraping a rough wooden dish in which some meagre food had recently been cooked. Suddenly, one of the black boys, enraged by something said by one of his white companions, seized the knife and struck the lad over the head. One of the oakum-pickers called out to prevent him, but it was too late. Blood was flowing from the gash in the white boy's head.

Captain Delano turned to Don Benito in amazement. 'What does this mean?'

'It was nothing,' the pale Spaniard muttered dully. 'Merely sport.'

'Pretty serious sport, if you ask me,' Captain Delano retorted. 'If that kind of thing had happened on board the *Bachelor's Delight*, it would have been punished instantly.'

At these words, Don Benito turned on Captain Delano with one of his sudden staring half-lunatic looks. Then he relapsed into a state of torpor and answered, 'Doubtless, doubtless.'

Captain Delano felt sorry for him and wondered whether he was one of those paper captains he had known who made a point of ignoring what they had no power to control.

There was nothing sadder, he reflected, than a commander who had command in name only.

'Don't you think, Don Benito,' he said, glancing towards the oakum-picker who had attempted to intervene, 'that it would be a good idea to keep all your Africans employed? The younger ones especially need to be kept busy. It doesn't matter how useless the task may be or what state the ship is in. I remember once I kept men on my quarter-deck making mats for my cabin, at a time when I feared that my ship was in danger of being sunk. For three days we were in the grip of a violent gale and could do nothing but drive helplessly before it. Mats, men and all could easily have been gone forever. But I kept my sailors at it.'

'Doubtless, doubtless,' murmured Don Benito.

Captain Delano glanced again at the oakum-pickers and then at the hatchet-polishers nearby. 'But I see you keep at least some of your people employed.'

'Yes,' Don Benito replied vacantly.

Captain Delano pointed to the oakum-pickers. 'Those old men there, shaking their heads from their pulpits, they seem to act the part of old schoolmasters to the rest of them, even if their warnings are not heeded at times. Have they taken this duty on themselves, Don Benito, or have you appointed them to be, as it were, shepherds to your flock of black sheep?'

'Whatever posts they fill, I appointed them,' Don Benito replied sharply. He seemed to suspect that Captain Delano was mocking him and resented it.

'And these others, these Ashanti conjurors here,' Captain Delano continued. Rather uneasily, he eyed the brandished steel of the hatchet-polishers where in places it had been brought to a shine. 'This seems a curious business they are at, Don Benito?'

The Spaniard explained. 'Our general cargo which was not thrown overboard in the gales we met was much damaged by brine. Since coming into calm weather, I have had several cases of knives and hatchets brought up daily for

23

overhauling and cleaning.'

'Very sensible, Don Benito. I presume you are part owner of the ship and its cargo. Though I doubt whether the slaves are yours, are they?'

'I own everything you see,' Don Benito replied impatiently, 'except the main body of the slaves. They belonged to my late friend, Alexandro Aranda.'

As he spoke this name, Don Benito broke down. His knees shook, and his servant had to support him.

Captain Delano could guess the reason for such unusual emotion. To confirm whether or not he was right, he said after a pause, 'And may I ask, Don Benito, whether your friend whose loss so affects you accompanied his slaves at the outset of the voyage? You did mention earlier that you had some cabin-passengers.'

'Yes.'

'And he died of the fever?'

'He died of the fever. Oh, could I but —'

Don Benito broke off. His whole body was trembling.

'Pardon me,' Captain Delano said, speaking lowly, 'but I think I can understand why you feel your grief so deeply. The same kind of thing has happened to me. I too have suffered the loss of a dear friend, my own brother, at sea. Had I been sure his spirit was safe and well, I could have endured its departure like a man. But to think of that honest eye, that honest hand — both of which had so often met mine — and that warm heart, all, all cast overboard to the sharks like scraps to the dogs! It was then I made a vow. I would never have on board with me as a fellow passenger any man I loved unless I also had with me everything necessary to embalm his body in the event of his death. Then I could ensure that he was buried on shore. If your friend's remains were now on board this ship, Don Benito, you would not be so deeply upset by the mention of his name.'

'On board this ship?' echoed Don Benito. Then, with horrified gestures as though directed against some ghostly figure, he fell unconscious into the supportive arms of his attendant. The servant made a silent appeal to Captain Delano as though begging him not to speak any more about a subject that so distressed his master.

Captain Delano was somewhat pained by Don Benito's reaction. Poor man, he thought, he must have a superstitious nature and believe that goblins inhabit the dead body of a man. Just like those people who believe that ghosts take over abandoned houses. How differently men react. In a similar case, it would give me a solemn satisfaction to know that the body of a dead friend was whole and safe. But the merest suggestion of such a thing sends this Spaniard into a fit. I wonder what poor Alexandro Arando would say if he could see his friend now. No doubt on previous voyages when Alexandro was for months left behind, Don Benito longed and longed to see him. Yet here he is, overcome by terror, at the very thought of having him anywhere near him.

At that moment, one of the grizzled oakum-pickers struck the forecastle bell proclaiming ten o'clock. The dreary grave-yard toll, which showed that the bell had a flaw, broke the leaden calm.

At the same time, Captain Delano's attention was caught by the moving figure of a gigantic black man. He was emerging from the general crowd below and slowly advancing towards the elevated poop. He had an iron collar about his neck. From this hung a chain which was bound three times round his body. The last links of this were padlocked together at a broad band of iron round his waist.

'Atufal moves just like a mute at a funeral,' the servant murmured.

The man mounted the steps of the poop. He stood there, silent and unflinching, like a brave prisoner brought up to receive sentence, and faced Don Benito who had now recovered from his attack.

At the first glimpse of his approach, Don Benito had started. A resentful shadow had swept across his face. His white lips had glued together as though with a sudden memory of useless rage.

This is some stubborn mutineer, Captain Delano thought. As he surveyed the huge muscular body of the African, he couldn't help admiring its power and strength.

'See, master, he awaits your question,' the servant said.

Thus reminded, Don Benito nervously averted his glance as though to shun the rebellious response that he anticipated. In a disconcerted voice, he asked, 'Atufal, will you ask my pardon now?'

The man was silent.

'Again, master,' murmured the servant, at the same time reprimanding his countryman with his eye. 'Again, master. He will submit to master yet.'

'Answer,' said Don Benito, still keeping his glance turned away. 'You have but to say the word "pardon", and your chains shall be removed.'

At this, the man slowly raised both arms. There was a clanking of links as he let them fall lifelessly to his side and bowed his head. It was as though he were saying, 'No, I am content.'

'Go,' said Don Benito, holding in an emotion that it was impossible to decipher.

The man obeyed, departing as slowly and solemnly as he had arrived.

'Excuse me, Don Benito,' said Captain Delano, 'but I am most surprised by what has just happened. Can you please explain what it was about?'

'That man alone of all those on board has cause me offence, in a deep and particular way. I have had him put in chains. I —'

Here Don Benito paused. He put his hand to his head as though it were swimming, or as though a sudden confusion in his memory had come over him. His servant glanced reassuringly at him, and this seemed to restore him. He proceeded.

'I could not have him whipped. Not someone with such a

noble bearing as that. But I told him he must ask my pardon.
As yet he has not done so. Until he submits, I have
commanded that he appears before me every two hours.'

'And how long has this been going on?'

'Some sixty days.'

'And is he obedient in everything else? And respectful?'

'Yes.'

'Then I must say,' Captain Delano broke out excitedly,
'he has a royal spirit in him, this man.'

'He may have some right to it,' Don Benito returned
bitterly. 'He says he was king in his own land.'

'Yes,' the servant put in, 'those slits in Atufal's ears once
held wedges of gold. But poor Babo here was only a slave in
his own land. A black man's slave he was, and now he is a
white man's slave.'

Captain Delano was somewhat annoyed by the attendant's familiarity in interrupting the conversation in this
way. He examined the servant curiously and then glanced
inquiringly at his master. But as though used to being
informal with each other, neither servant nor master
appeared to understand Captain Delano's pointed glances.

'Please tell me,' Captain Delano continued, 'what was
Atufal's offence, Don Benito? If it was nothing very serious,
then my advice would be to release him from his penalty.
Especially as he seems to behave in a very docile way. And
also out of a natural respect for the spirit he shows.'

'No, no. Master will never do that,' the servant murmured to himself. 'Proud Atufal must first ask master's
pardon. The slave there carries the padlock, but the master
here carries the key.'

His attention thus directed, Captain Delano now noticed
for the first time a key that hung suspended by a slender
silken cord from Don Benito's neck. At once, interpreting
the servant's muttered words, he guessed the key's purpose.
He smiled and said, 'So, Don Benito, padlock and key. They
are indeed significant symbols.'

Don Benito bit his lip and faltered.

Captain Delano had intended his remark to be a playful allusion to the neat and concrete manner in which Don Benito's power over the black man was displayed. He was a man of such natural simplicity that he was incapable of making a sly comment or being ironic. Yet Don Benito, perhaps because of his depressed state, seemed to take offence. He seemed to find some kind of malicious purpose in the remark. He seemed to see it as a reflection on his failure to break down the stubborn determination of the slave.

Captain Delano was upset that Don Benito should interpret his words in this way, but he could not think how to put the situation right. Instead, he moved onto another subject of conversation.

But Don Benito was more than ever withdrawn, as though digesting to the last dregs the supposed offensive remark. Conversation was difficult. At last, Captain Delano too became less talkative. He did not wish to be, but there was apparently no alternative. He was oppressed by what seemed to be the secret vindictiveness of this extraordinarily sensitive Spaniard. He himself, being of a totally opposite disposition, refrained from showing or feeling any resentment. If he became silent, it was only because Don Benito's silence was contagious.

Chapter 5
Suspicions Grow

Shortly afterwards, the Spaniard, assisted by his servant, rather discourteously walked away from Captain Delano. This move could have been taken as the idle whim of bad temper. But there seemed to be more to it than that. Master and servant, lingering round the corner of the elevated skylight, began whispering together in low voices. Captain Delano found this very unpleasant.

And it wasn't only that. The Spaniard's moody attitude had had at times a certain delicate grandeur about it, but now it looked merely undignified. And as for the servile familiarity of the servant, that had lost its earlier charm and any sense of simple-hearted attachment it might once have had.

Captain Delano was embarrassed by the whole scene. He turned away to the other side of the ship. There, his glance accidentally fell on a young Spanish sailor. He had a coil of rope in his hand and had just stepped from the deck to the first round of the mizzen-rigging. Perhaps the man would not have been particularly noticeable were it not for the fact that he seemed to be behaving rather oddly. There was a sort of subdued eagerness about his actions. As he ascended to one of the yards, he kept his eye fixed on Captain Delano and then shifted his gaze in what appeared to be a perfectly natural progression to the two whisperers.

His own attention thus being drawn in that direction, Captain Delano gave a slight start. There was something about Don Benito's manner just then that suggested to Captain Delano that he himself was in part the subject of this whispered consultation. The idea was most disagreeable, and it hardly showed Don Benito in a flattering light.

Captain Delano found it difficult to explain the strange alternations in the behaviour of the Spanish captain. One moment he was courteous, and the next moment he was rude. There could be only two possible explanations. Either Don Benito was mad and not answerable for his actions, or else he was involved in some evil game of deceit.

The first idea had already crossed Captain Delano's mind, as it might well have done to any objective observer. But now that he was beginning to regard Don Benito's attitude as being deliberately offensive, the idea that he might be mad was more or less dismissed.

But if he was not a lunatic, what was he? Under the circumstances, would a gentleman behave the way this man was doing? Would even the most ill-bred fellow behave like this? The man was an imposter. He was some low-born adventurer masquerading as a sea-going nobleman. Yet he was so ignorant of the first requirements of gentlemanly behaviour that his present blatant discourtesy betrayed him. That strange extravagant display of manners, too, put on at other times suggested someone playing a part above his real social level.

Benito Cereno — Don Benito Cereno — a fine-sounding name. It was one too that was familiar — at least the surname was — to pursers and sea captains trading along the Spanish Main. It belonged to one of the most enterprising and extensive mercantile families in all those provinces. Several members of it had titles. It was like a Castilian equivalent of Rothschild, with a noble brother or cousin in every great trading town in South America.

The man who claimed to be Don Benito was in his early manhood, about twenty-nine or thirty. What better scheme for a rogue of talent and spirit than to pretend to be a member of a family such as that, involved in its maritime affairs? But this man was a pale invalid. Even so, that didn't prevent the possibility. Some confidence tricksters had been known to be so skilful that they could even give the appearance of being mortally ill. It could be that the Spaniard's outward appearance of feeble weakness was but a disguise for the most savage energies, and the velvet of his fine clothes like a kind of silky paw that concealed his fangs.

These fanciful ideas were not the result of concentrated thought. They came from without, not from within. They came suddenly too, all together like a hoar frost. And they vanished just as quickly as Captain Delano's sunny good-nature reasserted itself.

He glanced once more towards Don Benito. The Spaniard's face was now turned sideways towards him, visible above the skylight. Captain Delano was struck by the profile. The clear-cut line of it was refined by thinness — only to be expected as a result of ill-health. It was also refined about the chin by the beard. How could there ever have been any doubt about the matter? Don Benito was clearly a genuine off-shoot of the noble Cereno family.

Captain Delano was relieved by this thought. He now began to pace the poop in a casual way, humming a tune lightly to himself so as not to betray to Don Benito the doubts that had been going through his mind. He did not wish the Spaniard to be aware that he had suspected his rudeness of being something more sinister. Even less did he wish the Spaniard to know that he had suspected him of being involved in some kind of deception. Such mistrust on Captain Delano's part could still prove to be mere illusion.

He couldn't quite understand why this feeling of mistrust had come into his head. But there was no point in spending time trying to work out the reason. If he did that, he might regret it. He might allow Don Benito to gain some hint of the ungenerous ideas he had been speculating on. It was better, he decided, not to think any more about the matter at this stage.

Presently, Don Benito, still supported by his attendant, moved over towards Captain Delano. His pale face was twitching and overcast. He started to talk in a husky whisper. He seemed to be even more than usually embarrassed, and his voice had in it a strange sort of conspiratorial intonation.

'Señor, may I ask how long you have been anchored at this island?' he began.

'Oh, only a day or two, Don Benito.'

'And which port did you come from?'

'Canton.'

'And there, Señor, you exchanged your sealskins for teas and silks, I think you said?'

'Yes. Silks mostly.'

'And the balance you took in money, perhaps?'

Captain Delano fidgeted a little at this question, but he answered. 'Yes. Some silver. Not a great deal though.'

'Ah, well. May I ask how many men you have, Señor?'

Captain Delano started slightly, but again he replied. 'About five and twenty, all told.'

'And at present, Señor, they are all on board, I suppose?'

'All on board, Don Benito,' returned Captain Delano, pleased that this was the case.

'And will they all be on board tonight, Señor?'

There had been so many persistent questions that at this one Captain Delano could not help but look very earnestly at the questioner. Don Benito was unable to meet his glance. Instead, he dropped his eyes to the deck in a way that was both abject and agitated. His attitude was in marked contrast to that of his servant who was just then kneeling down to adjust one of Don Benito's shoe-buckles which had become loose. The man was looking up at his master's downcast face openly and frankly with an expression of humble curiosity.

Don Benito, still with a guilty shuffle, repeated his question. 'And — and will they all be on board tonight, Señor?'

'Yes, as far as I know,' returned Captain Delano. 'But no,' he went on, pulling himself together and seeing no reason why he should not tell the truth, 'some of them did talk of going off on another fishing expedition about midnight.'

'Your ships generally go — go more or less armed, I believe, Señor?'

'Oh, a six-pounder or two in case of emergency,' Captain Delano replied staunchly with a show of indifference. 'With a small stock of muskets, sealing-spears and cutlasses. That sort of thing, you know.'

As he made this response, Captain Delano again glanced at Don Benito, but the Spaniard's eyes were turned away. Awkwardly and abruptly, Don Benito changed the subject. He made some irritated reference to the calm, and then, without apology, once more withdrew to the opposite bulwarks with his attendant. The whispering between them was resumed.

Captain Delano wanted to think coolly about the conversation that had just occurred, but before he could do so, his attention was caught by the young Spanish sailor he had noticed earlier.

At that moment, the sailor was descending from the rigging. As he stooped over to spring in board to the deck, his voluminous unconfined shirt, made of coarse woollen material and much spotted with tar, opened out far down his chest to reveal a soiled undergarment. This seemed to be made of the finest linen and was edged at the neck with a narrow blue ribbon, sadly faded and worn.

Just then, the young sailor's eye was again fixed on the whisperers, and Captain Delano thought he observed some kind of significance in it. It was as though one of those silent secret signs the Freemasons use had that instant been interchanged.

His own glance was once more impelled in the direction of Don Benito, and, as before, he was forced to conclude that he himself was the subject of the whispered discussion. He paused. He became aware of the sound of the hatchet-polishers. He cast another swift sideways look at Don Benito and his attendant. They had the air of conspirators. The recent questionings and the incident of the young sailor brought Captain Delano's suspicions back with a rush that he could do nothing to prevent. But he was by nature himself so open and honest that he could not bear to think badly of others.

He put on a light-hearted and amused expression and rapidly crossed over to Don Benito and his attendant. 'Ah, Don Benito,' he said, 'your servant here seems high in your trust. He seems to be a sort of privy-counsellor in fact.'

At this, the servant looked up with a good-natured grin. But the master started as though he had been bitten by a snake. It was a moment or two before the Spaniard could recover himself sufficiently to reply. When he at last did so, it was with a cold restraint. 'Yes, Señor, I have trust in Babo.'

Here Babo changed his previous grin which had been like that of an amiable animal into an intelligent smile. He eyed his master gratefully.

Don Benito went on standing there, silent and reserved. Captain Delano could not make out whether this was unintentional or meant deliberately to hint that his presence was unwelcome. He had no wish to appear uncivil himself, even when faced with incivility. He made some trivial remark and moved away.

Again and again, he turned over in his mind the mysterious behaviour of the Spanish captain.

He had descended from the poop, and wrapped in thought, was passing near a dark hatchway leading down into the steerage, when some movement there caught his attention. He looked closer to see what it was that had moved. At the same instant, there was a sparkle in the shadowy hatchway. He saw one of the Spanish sailors who was prowling there hurriedly place his hand in the opening of his shirt. It was as though he were hiding something. Before the man could have been certain who it was that was passing, he had slunk below out of sight. But Captain Delano had seen enough of him to recognise that it was the same young sailor he had noticed earlier in the rigging.

What was it that had sparkled like that, Captain Delano wondered. It wasn't a lamp or a match or a live coal. Could it have been a jewel? But how could it come about that sailors had jewels? Or silk-trimmed under-shirts, come to that? Had he been robbing the trunks of the dead cabin-passengers? But if so, he would hardly wear one of the stolen articles here on board ship.

Captain Delano pondered further. What if that had indeed been a secret sign that he saw passing between this suspicious fellow and his captain a short time before? He felt uneasy. If he could only be certain that his senses had not deceived him, then —

Here, moving, from one suspicion to another, he turned over in his mind the strange questions that had been put to him concerning his ship. By a curious coincidence, as each point was recalled, the black wizards of Ashanti struck up with their hatchets. It was like an ominous commentary on the white stranger's thoughts. Disturbed as he was by such riddles and omens, it was only natural that even the most trusting person should feel some unpleasant misgivings.

The ship had now fallen helplessly into a current and was drifting seaward with increasing speed. The *Bachelor's Delight* was hidden behind a projection of land. As he observed this, Captain Delano began to tremble at thoughts which he barely dared confess to himself. Above all, he began to feel a fearful dread of Don Benito. And yet . . .

He roused himself, breathed in deeply, settled his feet firmly on the deck, and coolly considered it. What did all these wild thoughts amount to?

If Don Benito had any sinister scheme, it must involve not

so much him (Captain Delano) as his ship (the *Bachelor's Delight*). Therefore, the fact that the two ships were, at present at least, drifting apart would hinder rather than help any such scheme. Under such circumstances, the suspicion that some evil purpose was intended had to be mistaken.

In any case, wasn't it absurd, a thousand times absurd, to think that a vessel in distress would have any intention of attacking another — a vessel almost dismanned of her crew by sickness, a vessel whose inmates were parched for water? And the commander. Wasn't it absurd that either he or those under him should cherish any desire other than speedy relief and refreshment?

But then again, on the other hand, might not the general distress of the ship, and the thirst in particular, be all just a show? And might not the whole Spanish crew, most of whom it was alleged had perished, be lurking that very moment in the hold? There were cases of fiends in human form gaining entry into lonely dwellings on the pretence of begging for a cup of cold water and staying there until they had committed some dark deed. And among the Malay pirates, it was not unusual for them to lure ships after them into their treacherous harbours, or to entice boarders from an enemy at sea by the appearance of thinly manned or empty decks, while below there prowled a hundred spears with yellow arms ready to thrust them up through the mats.

Not that Captain Delano entirely believed such stories. He had heard of them, and now they returned to haunt his mind. The present intention of the *San Dominick* was to anchor in the harbour of St Maria. There she would be near his own vessel. When she had gained that spot, was it not possible that the *San Dominick*, like a slumbering volcano, might then suddenly let loose energies that were now hidden?

He recalled Don Benito's manner while telling his story. There was a kind of sullen hesitancy and deviousness about it. It was exactly the manner of someone making up his story for evil purposes as he goes along. But if that story was not true, what was the truth? That the ship had come unlawfully into Don Benito's possession? But many of the details of Don Benito's story had been corroborated, particularly the references to the more distressing events such as the deaths among the seamen, the prolonged beating about that the ship underwent, the persistent calms that had to be endured, the suffering from thirst which still continued. All of these points, as well as others, had been corroborated not just by the wailing cries of the general mob on board, both white and black, but also by the expressions that Captain Delano saw on every human feature. It seemed impossible that such things could be counterfeited. If Don Benito's story was a complete invention, then every soul on board, down to the youngest African girl, was his carefully drilled recruit in the plot. Such a conclusion was incredible. And yet, if there were grounds for doubting Don Benito's truthfulness, such a conclusion was perfectly possible.

Then there were those questions Don Benito had put to him. There indeed one might have reason to pause. Was it not the case that they seemed to have been put with much the same objective that a burglar or assassin might have when he reconnoitres the walls of a house in daylight? But if your intention was evil, would you really ask such information openly of the person most in danger? It seemed an unlikely way of going about things. It was absurd, then, to suppose that those questions had been prompted by some evil purpose.

And so, Don Benito's behaviour which in this instance had raised Captain Delano's alarms was now the very thing that dispelled them. In short, most of Captain Delano's suspicions and uneasiness, though apparently reasonable at the time, were now with equal apparent reason dismissed.

At last, he began to laugh to himself at his former fears. He laughed at the strange ship which by her appearance had gone some way towards supporting them. And he laughed too at the odd-looking Africans — particularly those old scissors-grinders, the Ashantis, and those bed-ridden old knitting women, the oakum-pickers — and almost at the dark Spaniard himself, the hobgoblin at the centre of it all.

As for the rest of it, whatever serious doubts there might have been could easily be explained away by the thought that most of the time the poor invalid scarcely knew what he was doing. And this applied to whether the man was sulking in deep depression or putting idle questions that had neither sense nor object. Evidently, for the present, the man was not fit to be entrusted with the ship. It was possible yet that Captain Delano might have to plead with Don Benito for his own good to allow him to send the ship to Conception under the charge of his second mate, a reliable man and a good navigator. Such a plan would be just as beneficial for Don Benito as for the *San Dominick*. Relieved from all anxiety, keeping wholly to his cabin, the sick man under the good nursing of his servant would probably be largely restored to health by the end of the voyage. He could then also be restored to his command.

Such were Captain Delano's thoughts. They helped to calm him. There was a difference between the idea of Don Benito's wickedly plotting Captain Delano's fate and Captain Delano's nonchalantly arranging Don Benito's. Even so, it was with some relief that Captain Delano presently observed the whale-boat in the distance. It had taken longer to return than expected because of delays while alongside the *Bachelor's Delight* and because of the continual drifting away of the *San Dominick*.

The Africans also noticed the advancing speck. Their shouts attracted the attention of Don Benito. With a return of courtesy, the Spaniard approached Captain Delano and expressed his pleasure at the coming of some supplies, even though these were inevitably bound to be few in number and unlikely to last long.

'I must thank you for this assistance,' Don Benito said.

'It is the least I can do,' returned Captain Delano.

As he spoke, his attention was drawn to something taking place on the deck below. The crowd had climbed the landward bulwarks, anxiously watching the approaching boat. In the crush, one of the sailors seemed to have accidentally got in the way of two of the Africans, who violently pushed the sailor aside and, when he protested, dashed him to the deck in spite of earnest cries from the oakum-pickers.

'Don Benito,' said Captain Delano quickly, 'do you see what is going on there? Look!'

But Don Benito did not reply. Seized by his cough, he staggered with both hands to his face on the point of falling. Captain Delano stretched out his hand to support him, but the servant was quicker. With one hand he held his master up and with the other put the cordial to his master's lips. When Don Benito had recovered, the man withdrew his support. He slipped aside a little, but dutifully remained within the call of a whisper.

Captain Delano was impressed. The attendant showed such discretion that any blame Captain Delano might have levelled at him previously for improper conduct in those whispered discussions was now totally wiped away. It demonstrated too that if the servant were to blame, it was more likely to be his master's fault than his own, because it was clear that when he was left to himself, he could behave in a fitting manner as he was now doing.

His attention thus distracted from the disturbance he had witnessed on the deck below to a sight that was much more pleasing, Captain Delano couldn't help congratulating Don Benito again on possessing such a servant.

'He may be a little too forward now and then,' Captain Delano went on, 'but he must on the whole be invaluable to an invalid like yourself. Tell me,' he added with a smile, 'I should like to have your man here as my own servant. What will you take for him? Would fifty doubloons be a reasonable sum?'

'Master wouldn't part with Babo for a thousand

doubloons,' murmured the servant, overhearing the offer. He seemed to have thought that Captain Delano was being serious. It was typical of that strange vanity that faithful slaves have. Appreciated by his master, he was scornful that a stranger should value him at such a paltry sum.

Don Benito himself, not fully recovered from his fit, was wracked once more by his cough, and could only utter a few broken words in reply.

His physical distress increased and seemed to affect his mind. So much so, that the servant gently assisted his master below, as if to screen such a sad spectacle from the eyes of others.

Chapter 6
Various Encounters

Left to himself, Captain Delano looked around him for some way of whiling away the time until his boat arrived. He thought of having a pleasant word with some of the few Spanish sailors that were about. But then he recalled something that Don Benito had said about their poor conduct. He changed his mind. As a shipmaster, he did not feel inclined to give moral support to seamen who had shown cowardice or disloyalty.

While these thoughts were crossing his mind, he stood with his eye directed forward towards that handful of sailors. Suddenly he was aware that some of them were also staring at him in a way that appeared to have some kind of significance. He rubbed his eyes and looked again. But again he seemed to see the same thing. Once more, the old suspicions returned, in a new form this time, and more vaguely than before. But because Don Benito was not present, he felt less panic.

In spite of the bad account he had been given of the sailors, Captain Delano decided straightaway to talk to one of them. He descended from the poop and made his way through the crowd of Africans. As he did so, there was a strange cry from the oakum-pickers. The crowd, as though prompted by this, pushed each other aside and divided to make way for him. But then, as if curious to find out why Captain Delano was coming to visit their part of the ship, they closed in behind him in reasonable order and followed him. It was as though he were making a kind of royal progress, proclaimed by mounted heralds and escorted by a Kaffir guard of honour.

Assuming a good-humoured off-hand air, Captain Delano continued to advance. Now and then he spoke a cheerful word to the men nearest him, while he curiously surveyed the white faces that were sparsely mixed in with the black ones here and there. They were like stray white pawns that had daringly penetrated the ranks of an opponent's chess-men.

While wondering which of them to select for his purpose, Captain Delano chanced to observe a sailor seated on the deck engaged in tarring the strap of a large block. A circle of Africans squatted round him inquisitively eyeing the process.

The mean employment of the man was in contrast with something superior in his appearance. His hand, black with constantly thrusting it into the tar-pot held for him by an African, did not seem to match his face which would have been very fine but for its haggardness. It was impossible to say whether or not this haggardness indicated some kind of criminal mind. Because both innocence and guilt when afflicted by mental pain can mark the face with signs of suffering. Just as intense heat and cold, though unlike, produce similar sensations.

Such thoughts did not pass through Captain Delano's mind at the time, even though he was a charitable man. Instead, another idea occurred to him. In observing the sailor's extreme haggardness and the way his dark eyes were turned away as though troubled or ashamed, he recalled the ill opinion Don Benito had expressed of his crew. Unconsciously he was influenced by the general belief that suffering and shame are invariably connected with vice, not virtue.

He concluded that if there were indeed any wickedness on board that ship, then the sailor he had observed was bound to have fouled his hand in it — just as he now fouled it in the pot of tar. Under no circumstances would he speak to him. He would find someone else.

He turned away and approached an old Spanish sailor on the windlass. He was wearing ragged red breeches and a dirty night-cap. His cheeks were furrowed and tanned. He had whiskers as dense as thorn hedges. Seated between two sleepy-looking Africans, this sailor like his younger shipmate was employed upon some rigging, splicing a cable. His sleepy-looking companions performed the inferior function of holding the outer parts of the ropes for him.

On Captain Delano's approach, the man immediately hung his head lower than it had been, lower than the level necessary for the work he was doing. He gave the impression that he wanted anyone observing to think that he was absorbed with more than usual concentration on his task.

When Captain Delano spoke to him, the sailor glanced up. But there was something furtive and nervous about his expression which did not go with his weather-beaten face. It was as if a grizzly bear, instead of growling and biting, should smile and look bashful.

Captain Delano asked him a number of questions about the voyage. He deliberately asked about points in Don Benito's account which had not already been corroborated by those impulsive cries that had greeted him when he first came on board. His questions were answered briefly and confirmed all that remained to be confirmed of the story.

The Africans about the windlass joined in with the old sailor. But as they became more talkative, he grew more and more silent. In the end, he looked quite sullen and appeared to sulk and be unwilling to answer any more questions. Yet, all the while, there was this strange impression about him of a fierce bear with a gentle face.

Captain Delano felt embarrassed. It was impossible to talk naturally with someone like this who seemed so divided within himself. He glanced round in search of someone more promising to talk to, but found no one. So he asked the Africans politely to make way for him. This they did, with various grins and grimaces, and he returned to the poop. He felt a little strange at first, he couldn't tell why. But on the whole, he was reassured, and his confidence in Don Benito was restored.

He reflected on what had just happened. The old whiskered sailor had betrayed only too clearly how guilty his conscience was. There could be no doubt about it. When he saw me coming, he was afraid I was going to give him a few sharp words, having been told by his captain how badly the crew had behaved. That was why he lowered his head. And yet — and yet, now that I think of it, that old sailor if I'm not mistaken was one of those who seemed to stare at me so earnestly a while back. Ah, these currents seem to stir one's head round almost as much as they do the ship.

And then his attention was drawn to another sight, something altogether more pleasant and sociable. It was the figure of a sleeping African woman which he could partly see through the lace-work of some rigging. She was lying with her youthful limbs casually spread out under the lee of the bulwards. She looked like a doe resting in the shade of a woodland rock. Her wide-awake baby, like a fawn, was sprawling at her breasts. It was stark naked, its little black body half lifted from the deck, where it fell across its mother's. Its hands, like two paws, fought hard to climb on top of her. Its mouth and nose rooted without success to get at her nipples. As it struggled, it gave forth an annoyed half-grunt which blended with the steady snore of the mother.

At length, the child's activity roused her. She started up, directly facing Captain Delano though at a distance. But she appeared not at all concerned at being observed in the state she was in. She caught the child up delightedly, full of motherly love, and covered it with kisses.

Captain Delano was touched. Here was simple nature, he

thought, pure tenderness and love.

The incident prompted him to look more closely at the other women than he had done before. He was pleased by what he saw. Like most uncivilized women, they seemed both tender of heart and strong of body. They were equally ready to die for their babies or fight for them. They were as natural as leopardesses, yet as loving as doves. Ah, thought Captain Delano, perhaps these are some of the very women the explorer Ledyard saw in Africa and of whom he gave such a noble account.

The sight of the women behaving so naturally helped to strengthen Captain Delano's sense of confidence and make him feel more relaxed. He looked to see how his boat was getting on, but it was still a long way off. He turned to see if Don Benito had returned, but he had not.

To give himself a change of scene and to have the pleasure of being able to observe the approaching boat more conveniently, he stepped over into the mizzen-chains and clambered his way into the starboard quarter-gallery. This was one of those abandoned Venetian-looking water-balconies he had noticed during his arrival. It was a secluded place cut off from the deck.

As his foot pressed the half-damp half-dry sea-mosses that matted the floor, a faint breeze came to fan his cheeks. It was a mere puff of a breeze that came without warning and vanished again like a ghost. Captain Delano's glance fell on the row of small round shutters on the port-holes. They were all closed and looked like the eyes of the dead weighed down with copper coins to keep them shut. The state-cabin door which had once communicated with the gallery, just as the shuttered port-holes had once looked out on it, was now sealed up fast like a coffin lid. The panels of the door were purple-black from being tarred over.

All these things made Captain Delano think of the time when the state-cabin and the state-balcony had resounded to the voices of the Spanish King's officers, and the figures of the daughters of the viceroy of Lima had perhaps leaned where he now stood. As these and other images flitted through his mind, as the light breeze did through the calm, he felt a vague uneasiness gradually rise within him. It was like the unrest that someone alone at noon on the prairie might feel from the very stillness around him.

Captain Delano leaned across the carved balustrade and again looked off towards his boat. But he found his eye attracted by the ribbon grass trailing along the ship's water-line. It was straight as a border of green hedge. There were areas like flower beds of sea-weed, broad ovals and crescents, floating near and far, with what seemed like formal alleys in between, crossing the terraces formed by the swell of the sea, and sweeping round as if leading to the grottoes below. And overhanging all was the balustrade by his arm, partly stained with pitch and partly embossed with moss, which seemed like the charred ruin of some summer-house in a grand garden that had long been left to run to waste.

In trying to break one charm, Captain Delano found himself caught up by another. Although he was on the open sea, he felt as though he were in some far inland country. He was like a prisoner in some deserted château, left to stare at the empty grounds and peer out at vague roads down which no wagon or traveller passed.

But such imaginings were somewhat disturbed when his eye fell on the corroded main-chains. They were of an antiquated style, heavy and rusty in link, shackle and bolt, and seemed even more suitable for the ship's present business than the one for which she had been built.

Just then, Captain Delano thought he saw something moving near the chains. He rubbed his eyes and looked hard. There were groves of rigging hanging about the chains. And there, peering from behind a great stay, like an Indian from behind a pine tree, was a Spanish sailor. He was holding a marlinspike in his hand. He made some kind of gesture towards the balcony. But he left the gesture unfinished, and immediately, as if alarmed by some advancing step along the deck within, vanished into the recesses of the forest of ropes, like a poacher.

What did this mean? The man had tried to communicate some message, without anyone else knowing, without his captain knowing. Could it be that the secret concerned something that was unfavourable to his captain? Were Captain Delano's previous misgivings about to be proved true?

Or had he, in the haunted mood he was in, mistaken the meaning of the man's gesture? It might not have had any significance. It might have been simply a random movement the man made without anything behind it while he was busy with the stay — repairing it perhaps.

Confused again in his thought, Captain Delano searched the sea for his boat. But it was temporarily hidden by a rocky spur of the island. As he bent forward eagerly, watching for the first sight of its prow shooting back into vision, the balustrade gave way before him like charcoal. If he hadn't clutched an outreaching rope, he would have fallen into the sea.

The crash and fall of the rotten fragments were feeble and hollow, but they must have been overheard. Captain Delano glanced up. One of the old oakum-pickers had slipped from his perch to an outside boom and was peering down at him with solemn curiosity. Below the old man and invisible to him was the Spanish sailor again. He was crouched down and was checking what had happened from a port-hole, like a fox from the mouth of its den.

There was something about the man's attitude that caused a mad idea to dart into Captain Delano's mind. Don Benito had pleaded illness to withdraw below. Could that have been just a pretence? Perhaps he was busy there working on his plot. The sailor might somehow have got to know about it. His intention might have been to warn Captain Delano of it. The sailor might have been moved to do this out of gratitude for some kind word Captain Delano had said to him on first boarding the ship.

It was possible that Don Benito had foreseen something of

this sort happening. That could have been the reason why he had spoken so badly of his sailors while praising the Africans. Though in fact the sailors seemed reasonably well behaved whereas the Africans were not.

But then, white men were by nature shrewder than black men. Wasn't it likely that someone who intended evil would speak well of people who were too stupid to see his wickedness, and speak badly of those who were intelligent enough to know what was going on? It was quite possible.

But if the white sailors had dark suspicions about Don Benito, could then Don Benito somehow be in league with the Africans? But they were too stupid. Besides, who ever heard of a white man who was such a traitor to his race as to link himself with Africans?

Lost in these difficult thoughts, as though in a maze, and in earlier thoughts that came back to him, Captain Delano walked back to the deck. He was uneasily advancing along it when he observed a new face. It was an aged sailor seated cross-legged near the main hatchway. His skin was shrunk up with wrinkles like a pelican's empty pouch. His hair was frosted. The expression on his face was serious and composed. His hands were full of ropes which he was working into a hard knot. Some Africans around him helpfully dipped the strands in and out for him as the task required.

Captain Delano crossed over to him and stood examining the knot in silence. By a not unpleasant transition, his mind passed from its own entanglements to those of the rope. He had never seen such an intricate knot on an American ship, or indeed on any other. The old man looked like some ancient priest weaving those impenetrable Gordian knots of mythology. The knot seemed to be a combination of double-bowline-knot, treble-crown-knot, back-handed-well-knot, knot-in-and-out-knot, and jamming-knot.

At last, puzzled to understand the meaning of such a knot, Captain Delano asked, 'What are you knotting there, my man?'

'The knot,' the old sailor replied briefly without looking up.

'So it seems, but what is it for?'

'For someone else to undo,' the old man muttered back, plying his fingers harder than ever. The knot was now nearly complete.

While Captain Delano stood watching him, the old man suddenly threw the knot towards him, saying, 'Undo it, cut it, quick.' The words were spoken in broken English, the first Captain Delano had heard on board the ship. They were spoken in a low tone and very rapidly, so that the slow long words in Spanish that preceded and followed them almost acted as a cover for the brief words of English in between.

For a moment, Captain Delano stood silent, knot in hand with a similar knot in his mind. The old man, paying no more attention to him, busied himself with other ropes.

Shortly afterwards, Captain Delano became conscious of a slight stir behind him. Turning, he saw the chained giant, Atufal, standing quietly there. The next moment, the old sailor rose. He muttered to himself and moved to the forward part of the ship, accompanied by his subordinate followers. There, he was soon lost in the crowd.

An elderly African now approached Captain Delano. He wore a cloth wrapped round his loins like a baby's napkin. His hair was sprinkled with white, and he had a learned air about him as if he were a lawyer.

'The old sailor is simple-minded,' the African informed Captain Delano in tolerable Spanish. He gave the captain a good-natured knowing wink. 'But he's harmless. He often plays these odd tricks. Please may I have the knot?' he went on. 'Because I am sure you do not wish to be troubled with it.'

Without thinking about it, Captain Delano handed the knot over. The man received it with a sort of bow. He turned his back and ferreted through the bundle of tied ropes like a customs officer searching for smuggled goods. Soon, with some African word which seemed to express contempt, he tossed the knot overboard.

Chapter 7
The Boat Arrives

Now all of this was very strange, Captain Delano thought, and he felt his stomach turn queasily. But like someone feeling a bout of seasickness coming on, he endeavoured to get rid of it by ignoring the symptoms. Once more, he looked out for his boat. To his delight, it was now again in view, leaving the rocky spur astern.

The joy he experienced on seeing the boat at first relieved his uneasiness and then removed it altogether. The boat called forth a thousand trustful associations which, contrasted with his previous suspicions, filled him with a light-hearted confidence. It could be seen clearly outlined, not as before half obscured by the haze. Its individual features could now be identified.

The boat was named *Rover*. Though it was now in strange seas, it had often pressed the beach of Captain Delano's home, having been brought there for repairs. It had lain there at the threshold to his house like a Newfoundland dog that was a familiar pet. Not only did the sight of it restore his confidence, but it also made him reproach himself and laugh at his earlier fears.

'How could I have had such thoughts? I, Amasa Delano — Jack of the Beach, as they called me when a lad. I can see myself now, satchel in hand, padding along the water-side to the school-house made from an old hulk. And going to pick berries with cousin Nat and the others. And am I to be murdered here at the ends of the earth on board a haunted pirate-ship by a horrible Spaniard? How absurd! Who would murder Amasa Delano? His conscience is clear. There is someone above who will protect him. How could you, Jack of the Beach! You are a child indeed, a child in his second childhood, old boy. I fear you are beginning to dote and dribble at the mouth.'

Light of heart and foot, Captain Delano stepped aft. There he was met by Don Benito's servant with a pleasant expression on his face that matched his own feelings.

'My master has recovered from the effects of his coughing fit,' the man informed him. 'He has ordered me to present his compliments to you, Don Amasa, his good guest, and to say that he will soon have the happiness to rejoin you.'

There now, do you mark that, Captain Delano again thought as he walked up and down the poop. What a donkey I was. This kind gentleman who here sends me his kind compliments, he, but ten minutes ago, dark-lantern in hand, was dodging round some old grind-stone in the hold, sharpening a hatchet for me, I thought. Well, well. I've often heard that these long calms have a morbid effect on the mind, though I never believed it before.

'Ha!' he exclaimed, glancing towards the boat. 'There's *Rover*. Good dog. With a white bone in her mouth. A pretty big bone though, it seems to me. What? Yes, she has fallen foul of the bubbling tide-rip there. It sets her the other way too for the moment. I must be patient.'

It was now almost noon, though from the greyness of everything it seemed to be getting towards dusk.

The calm continued. In the far distance, away from the influence of land, the leaden sea was like a body laid out and coffined, its course finished, its soul gone, dead. But the current from landward, where the ship was, increased. It was silently sweeping her further and further towards those sleeping waters beyond.

But Captain Delano was not dismayed by the present situation. From his knowledge of those latitudes, he still had hopes of a breeze, and a fair and fresh one, at any moment. He cheerfully counted on bringing the *San Dominick* safely into harbour before night. The distance the ship had drifted was nothing. With a good wind, it would be easy to undo sixty minutes of drifting in ten minutes of sailing.

Meanwhile, one moment turning to observe *Rover* fighting the tide-rip, and the next to see if Don Benito were approaching, Captain Delano continued his walk up and down the poop.

But gradually he began to feel annoyed at the delay of his boat. And then his annoyance merged into uneasiness. His eye fell continually on the strange crowd before and below him, as from a stage-box into the pit. By and by, he recognized there the face of the Spanish sailor who had seemed to beckon to him from the main-chains. The face now wore an expression of indifference, but something of Captain Delano's previous fears returned.

Ah, he thought, this is indeed like a fever. Because it has died down, it doesn't mean that it won't come back again.

He was ashamed at letting his misgivings rise once more, but he could not altogether prevent them. So, calling on his commonsense to help him, he came to a compromise.

Yes, this was a strange ship. It had a strange history too, and it had strange people on board. But that was all. There was nothing more to it than that.

To keep his mind from more worrying thoughts until his boat arrived, Captain Delano turned over and over, merely as a kind of mental exercise, some of the lesser peculiarities of the captain and crew. Among others, four curious points came back to him.

First, there was the affair of the Spanish lad assaulted with a knife by the slave boy, an act that Don Benito had shut his eyes to.

Second, there was the tyrannical way in which Don

Benito treated Atufal, a man of great dignity. It was as improper as it would be for a child to lead a sacred bull by the ring in its nose.

Third, there was the incident in which the two Africans threw the sailor to the deck, a piece of insolence passed over without so much as a reprimand.

Fourth, there was the cringeing submission of all the ship's lower orders, mostly Africans, to their master — as if they feared that the least negligence on their part would draw down punishment from this all-powerful tyrant.

When these points were put together like this, they seemed somewhat contradictory. But so what, thought Captain Delano, glancing towards the boat which was now much nearer — so what? Why, Don Benito is a very inconsistent commander. And he is not the first of his sort that I have seen. Though it is true that he is the worst.

But as a nation the Spaniards are all rather odd, Captain Delano went on in his thoughts. The very word 'Spaniard' has a curious conspiratorial Guy-Fawkish twang to it. And yet, I dare say, Spaniards in the main are as good people as any in Duxbury, Massachusetts.

Then he exclaimed aloud with pleasure. *Rover* had arrived at last.

The boat, with its welcome freight, touched the side. The Africans, on seeing the three water-casks in its bottom and a pile of wilted pumpkins in its bow, hung over the bulwarks, wild with joy. The oakum-pickers, waving their stiff arms about, tried to restrain them.

Don Benito now appeared with his servant. His arrival had perhaps been hastened by the noise. Captain Delano asked his permission to serve out the water so that all might get an equal share, and none might suffer harmful effects from drinking too much and more than his fair allowance.

But though this was a sensible request made out of consideration for Don Benito himself, it was received with what seemed like impatience. It was as if Don Benito was aware that he was a feeble commander. With the fury typical of those who are weak, he resented any interference and saw it as an insult. That, at least, was the way Captain Delano interpreted Don Benito's reaction.

In another moment, the casks were being hauled in. In the excitement, some of the Africans accidentally jostled Captain Delano where he stood by the gangway. Forgetting about Don Benito, Captain Delano instinctively ordered them to stand back. He spoke pleasantly but firmly. To support his words, he raised his hand in a gesture that was half joking and half threatening.

Instantly, they halted exactly where they were, remaining frozen like this for a few seconds while an unknown word ran from man to man among the perched oakum-pickers as though between the responsive posts of a telegraph. While Captain Delano's attention was fixed by this scene, the hatchet-polishers suddenly began to rise to their feet. Don Benito gave a sharp cry.

It was a signal from the Spaniard. Captain Delano was sure of it. He was about to be massacred. He made ready to spring for his boat. But then he paused.

The oakum-pickers had dropped down into the crowd with earnest cries. They began forcing every man back, both white and black. At the same time, they gestured to Captain Delano in a friendly, familiar, even playful way — as if telling him not to be a fool, as there was nothing to be worried about. Simultaneously, the hatchet-polishers resumed their seats, quietly like so many tailors. And at once it was as if nothing had happened. The work of hoisting in the casks began again, Spaniards and Africans singing as they worked at the tackle.

Captain Delano glanced towards Don Benito. The agitated invalid had collapsed into the arms of his servant and was now recovering and drawing himself up. As Captain Delano looked at this feeble figure, he could only marvel at the panic which had so suddenly taken him by surprise. How could he ever have supposed that such a commander with such a lack of self-command was going to bring about his murder?

When the casks were on deck, Captain Delano was handed a number of jars and cups by one of the steward's assistants. The man begged him, in the name of his captain, to do as he had proposed — dole out the water. This Captain Delano did impartially, in the true spirit of equality, serving the oldest Spaniard no better than the youngest African. After all, water is the most egalitarian element of all, and always seeks one level.

The only exception Captain Delano made was poor Don Benito whose health, if not his position, demanded an extra allowance. And it was he that Captain Delano served first, presenting him with a large pitcher full. But though he must have been suffering severely from thirst, the Spaniard would not drink a drop until he had made a number of solemn bows and salutes in return. The Africans who love displays like this greeted this exchange of courtesies with a great clapping of hands.

Two of the less wilted pumpkins were reserved for the captain's table. The rest were minced up on the spot for the others to eat. Captain Delano wanted to keep the soft bread, sugar and bottled cider for the Spaniards alone, and in particular Don Benito. But he objected, and Captain Delano was pleased by this generous gesture. As a result, mouthfuls were given all around to Spaniards and Africans. Except for one bottle of cider which Babo insisted on setting aside for his master.

It should here be pointed out that Captain Delano, as on the first visit, did not permit any of his own men to board the ship. He did not wish to add to the confusion on deck.

There was now a general sense of well-being on board, and all doubts and misgivings were forgotten. Captain Delano sent the boat back to the *Bachelor's Delight* with orders for all the hands that could be spared immediately to set about rafting casks to the watering-place and filling them. He still counted on a breeze within an hour or two at the latest, but he sent a message to his chief officer that if the unexpected happened and the ship was not brought to anchor by sunset, there was nothing to worry about. As there was to be a full moon that night, he himself would remain on board ready to act as pilot, whether the wind came soon or late.

Chapter 8
The Shave

As the two captains stood together, observing the departing boat, Captain Delano expressed his regrets that the *San Dominick* had no boats. The servant was busying himself in rubbing out a spot that he had just spied on his master's velvet sleeve.

It was true that the *San Dominick* had no boat. None, at least, but the unseaworthy old hulk of the long-boat. This lay like a pot turned upside down amidships. It was as warped as a camel's skeleton in the desert, and almost as bleached. With one of its sides a little tipped up, it made a kind of subterranean den for family groups, mostly women and small children. They could be seen some distance wtihin, squatting on old mats below, or perched above in the dark dome on the elevated seats. They looked like a sociable circle of bats sheltering in a friendly cave. Every now and then, black flights of naked boys and girls, three or four years old, darted in and out of the den's mouth.

'Now if you had three or four boats, Don Benito,' Captain Delano said, 'it would help a lot. You could use your Africans here to pull at the oars. Did you sail from port without boats, Don Benito?'

'They were smashed in the gales, Señor.'

'That was bad luck. Many men, too, you lost then. Boats and men. Those must have been hard gales, Don Benito.'

'Past all talking about,' said the Spaniard, and he cringed.

'Tell me, Don Benito,' continued Captain Delano with increased interest, 'tell me, were these gales immediately off the most extreme point of Cape Horn?'

'Cape Horn? Who spoke of Cape Horn?'

'You yourself did,' answered Captain Delano. 'When giving me an account of your voyage.' He was astonished at the way Don Benito had snapped at his words. 'You yourself, Don Benito, spoke of Cape Horn,' he repeated with emphasis.

Don Benito turned in a sort of stooping posture. He paused an instant, like someone about to plunge from one element to another, from air to water.

At that moment, a messenger-boy hurried by. He was engaged in his regular job of carrying the time from the cabin clock forward to the forecastle to have it struck at the ship's large bell.

'Master,' said the servant. He discontinued his work on the coat sleeve and addressed the Spaniard, who seemed to be in a trance, with a kind of timid apprehensiveness. He spoke like someone given a duty to perform which it was clear would irritate the very person who had imposed the duty and for whose benefit it was meant. 'Master told me, never mind where he was, or how occupied, always to remind him, to a minute, when shaving-time comes. Miguel has gone to strike the half-hour afternoon. It is *now*, master. Will master go into the cuddy?'

'Ah, yes,' answered Don Benito, starting as from dreams back to reality. Then he turned to Captain Delano. 'We shall resume our conversation before long.'

'Then if master means to talk more to Don Amasa,' said the servant, 'why not let Don Amasa sit by master in the cuddy, and master can talk, and Don Amasa can listen, while Babo here lathers and strops.'

'Yes,' said Captain Delano, approving of this suggestion, 'yes, Don Benito, unless you had rather not, I will go with you.'

'As you like, Señor.'

As the three of them went aft, Captain Delano could not help thinking that here was another example of the Spaniard's strange behaviour. How peculiar to insist on being shaved with such punctuality in the middle of the day. But it was more than likely that the servant's anxious concern for his master had something to do with it. A timely interruption such as this would serve to rouse his master from the mood that clearly was descending on him.

The place called the cuddy was a light deck-cabin formed by the poop, a sort of attic to the large cabin below. Part of it had formerly been the quarters of the officers. But since their death, all the partitionings had been taken down and the whole interior converted into one spacious and airy marine hall. The absence of fine furniture and the picturesque muddle of the various items it did contain gave it the appearance of the wide cluttered hall of some eccentric bachelor-squire in the country — the kind of person who hangs his shooting-jacket and tobacco-pouch on deer antlers, and keeps his fishing-rod, tongs and walking-stick jumbled up together in one corner.

The similarity was heightened by glimpses of the surrounding sea. It might even have been this that first brought the comparison to mind. Because in one respect, the wide expanses of the countryside and the wide expanses of the sea seem related.

The floor of the cuddy was matted. Overhead four or five old muskets were stuck into horizontal holes along the beams. On one side was an old claw-footed table lashed to the deck on which lay a thumbed prayer-book. Over it was a small plain crucifix attached to the bulk-head. Under the table were thrown one or two dented cutlasses and a hacked harpoon mixed up with some worn-out old rigging that looked like a heap of poor friars' girdles. There were also two long sharp-ribbed settees made of Malacca cane, black with age and as uncomfortable to look at as racks used by the Inquisition. A large misshapen armchair was furnished with a rough barber's head-rest at the back worked by a screw that gave it the appearance of some grotesque implement of torture.

An open flag-locker in one corner exposed a variety of coloured bunting, some rolled up, others half unrolled, still others tumbling out in disorder. Opposite it was a cumbrous wash-stand. It was made of black mahogany, all of one block, with a pedestal like a font. Over it was a railed shelf containing combs, brushes and other toilet gear. A torn hammock of stained matting swung nearby. The sheets were tossed about and the pillow was wrinkled up like a frowning forehead as if whoever slept there slept badly, visited alternately by sad thoughts and bad dreams.

The further side of the cuddy, overhanging the ship's stern, was pierced by three openings. These might have been windows or port-holes, through which men and cannon could peer, depending on whether they were socially or unsocially inclined. At present, neither men nor cannon were to be seen, though huge ring-bolts and other rusty iron fixtures on the woodwork suggested twenty-four pounders.

Glancing towards the hammock as he entered, Captain Delano said, 'You sleep here, Don Benito?'

'Yes, Señor, since we got into mild weather.'

'This seems a strange mixture, Don Benito,' added Captain Delano, looking round. 'A sort of dormitory, sitting-room, sail-loft, chapel, armoury and private closet all together.'

'Yes, Señor. Events have not been favourable to much order in my arrangements.'

Here, the servant with napkin on arm made a gesture as if to show that he was awaiting his master's pleasure. Don Benito indicated that he was ready. He sat down in the Malacca armchair. The servant drew one of the settees opposite for Captain Delano's convenience, and then began his work by throwing back his master's collar and loosening his cravat.

There is something in the African which makes him particularly fitting to have working about one's person, Captain Delano thought. Most Africans are natural valets and hairdressers. They take to the comb and brush as easily as they do to the castinets, and flourish them apparently with almost as much satisfaction. There is too a kind of smooth tact about them when so employed. They have a marvellous noiseless gliding briskness which is quite graceful in its way and very pleasing to watch. It is still more pleasing to be the person receiving such attentions.

Above all, they have the great gift of good-humour. This does not mean that they grin and laugh. Such behaviour would be unsuitable. But they have a certain easy cheerfulness which creates a kind of harmony of every glance and gesture. It is as though God had set every part of their bodies to some pleasant tune.

And there is yet more. They happily accept their positions because with their limited minds they are content with little. They are capable of a kind of quiet devotion that is sometimes found in people who are without question inferior.

When all of this is taken into account, it is not surprising that those hypochondriacs Dr Johnson and Lord Byron had black servants — perhaps in the same way that Don Benito, himself a hypochondriac, did. They took their serving men, Barber and Fletcher, to their hearts, almost to the exclusion of the entire white race. If men such as that, with morbid and cynical minds and a sour view of their fellow men, could like black people, then how must black people at their best appear to men with sympathetic minds?

When he was at peace with the world, Captain Delano's nature was not only kind but friendly and good-natured as well. At home, he had often taken a special pleasure in sitting at his door and watching some free man of colour at work or play. If on a voyage he chanced to have a black sailor among his crew, he was invariably on chatty and half-playful terms with him. In fact, like most men of a good and cheerful heart, he took to black men. This wasn't out of any moral sense of his duty to mankind. It was because he liked them. Just as other men take to and like Newfoundland dogs.

Up till now, in the circumstances in which he found himself on the *San Dominick*, he had had to repress this feeling. But in the cuddy, it was different. He felt freed from his former uneasiness. For various reasons, he was more sociably inclined than he had been all day. And then too, there was the sight of the servant, napkin on arm, busy and cheerful about his master, employed in the intimate act of shaving him. All of these things contributed to bring about the return of Captain Delano's old liking for Africans.

Among other things, he was amused by an example of that love of bright colours and fine shows that all Africans have. Babo casually took from the flag-locker a huge piece of bunting of all hues and tucked great quantities of it under his master's chin for an apron.

The mode of shaving among the Spaniards is a little different from what it is with other nations. They have a basin, specifically called a barber's basin, which is scooped out on one side so that the chin fits into it. This is held closely against the neck while lathering which is done not with a brush but with soap dipped in the water in the basin and rubbed on the face.

In the present instance, salt-water was used for lack of better, and the parts lathered were only the upper lip and low down under the throat, as all the rest was a cultivated beard.

These first steps were somewhat novel to Captain Delano. He sat curiously watching them so that no conversation took place. Don Benito too appeared disinclined to speak for the time being.

Setting down his basin, Babo searched among the razors

as though for the sharpest. When he had found the one he wanted, he gave it an additional edge by expertly stropping it on the firm smooth oily skin of his open palm. He then made a gesture as if to begin. But midway he stood suspended for an instant, one hand holding the razor in the air, the other dabbling professionally in the bubbling suds on the Spaniard's lean neck. The sight of the gleaming steel so close made Don Benito shudder nervously. The usual paleness of his skin was heightened by the lather, and that in turn was intensified by the blackness of the African's body.

Altogether, the scene was somewhat peculiar. At least it seemed so to Captain Delano. And as he saw the two figures thus positioned, he couldn't help thinking that the black man looked like an executioner and the white like a man at the block. But this was just one of those mad flashes, appearing and vanishing in a breath, that could perhaps afflict even the most sensible mind.

Meanwhile, the Spaniard's agitation had slightly loosened the bunting around him so that one broad fold of it swept like a curtain over the arm of the chair to the floor. On it was now revealed, amid a profusion of armorial bars and ground colours — black, blue and yellow — a closed castle in a blood-red field diagonal with a lion rampant in a white field.

'The castle and the lion,' exclaimed Captain Delano. 'Why, Don Benito, this is the flag of Spain you use here. It's just as well it's only I, and not the King, that sees this,' he added with a smile. He turned towards the servant. 'But it's all one, I suppose, so long as the colours are bright.' This playful remark caused the African to laugh.

'Now, master,' he said, readjusting the flag and pressing the head gently further back into the head-rest. 'Now, master,' and the steel glanced near the throat.

Again Don Benito shuddered faintly.

'You must not shake so, master. See, Don Amasa, master always shakes when I shave him. And yet master knows I never yet have drawn blood. Though it's true, if master will shake so, I may one of these times. Now, master,' he continued. 'And now, Don Amasa, please go on with your talk about the gale and all that. Master can hear, and between times, master can answer.'

'Ah, yes, these gales,' said Captain Delano. 'The more I think of your voyage, Don Benito, the more I wonder not at the gales, terrible though these must have been, but at the disastrous time that followed them. For, by your account, you have taken two months and more getting from Cape Horn to St Maria. This is a distance which I myself have sailed with a good wind in a few days. True, you had calms and long ones, but to be becalmed for two months, that is at least unusual. Why, Don Benito, if almost any other gentleman told me such a story, I should have been half inclined not to believe him.'

Here an uncontrollable spasm passed over the Spaniard's face, similar to that which had occurred shortly before on deck. Whether it was the start he gave, or a sudden awkward roll of the hull in the calm, or a momentary unsteadiness of the servant's hand, whatever it was, just then the razor drew blood. Spots of it stained the creamy lather under the throat. Immediately, Babo drew back the steel. Remaining in his professional attitude, back to Captain Delano, and face to Don Benito, he held up the trickling razor.

'See, master,' he said with a sort of half humorous sorrow. 'You shook so. Here's Babo's first blood.'

No sword drawn before James the First of England, no assassination attempt in the presence of that most timid of kings, could have produced a more terrified reaction than that which now appeared on Don Benito's face.

Poor man, thought Captain Delano. He is so nervous he can't even bear the sight of a little bit of blood spilled in shaving. How incredible that I should have imagined that this sick deranged man meant to spill all my blood when he can't even endure the sight of one little drop of his own. You must have been out of your mind to think so. Make sure you don't tell them about it when you get home, you idiot. I ask you, does he look like a murderer? He looks more as though he were about to be murdered. Never mind, let today's experience be a lesson to you.

While these thoughts were running through Captain Delano's mind, the servant took the napkin from his arm and said to Don Benito, 'Please answer Don Amasa, master, while I wipe this ugly stuff off the razor and strop it again.'

As he spoke, his face was turned half round so as to be visible to both captains. He seemed to be hinting from his expression that he was eager to get his master to go on with the conversation so as to distract his attention from the recent disturbing accident.

As if glad to snatch the relief being offered, Don Benito resumed. 'Not only did the calms continue for an unusually long time,' he told Captain Delano, 'but the ship had also become caught up in obstinate currents.'

And he added other things, some of which he had mentioned before, to explain why the ship had taken so long to get from Cape Horn to St Maria. Now and then, he put in a good word for the general conduct of the black people on board, praising them even more than he had done before. These details were not given in one speech. At convenient moments, the servant used his razor. So between intervals of shaving, Don Benito told his story and praised the Africans in a voice that was more than usually husky.

Captain Delano once more did not feel entirely at ease. In his view, there was something hollow about Don Benito's manner. This was matched by a similar falseness in the servant's silence. The idea flashed through him that it was possible that master and man were, for some unknown purpose, acting out some play before him intended to deceive him. Even the trembling of Don Benito's body might have been part of it. And there was evidence to support this suspicion of a secret understanding between them. There had been those whispered discussions previously mentioned.

But then, what could be the point of enacting this play of

the barber before him? Captain Delano speedily banished the notion as absurd. It was just a fanciful idea suggested by the theatrical effect presented by Don Benito decked out in his brightly-coloured bunting.

When the shaving was over, the servant busied himself with a small bottle of scented waters. He poured a few drops on Don Benito's head and diligently rubbed them in. The vigour with which he worked away at this task caused the muscles of his face to twitch rather strangely.

Next he went to work with comb, scissors and brush. He went round and round. smoothed a curl here, clipping an unruly whisker-hair there, giving a graceful sweep to the hair on the forehead. These and other spontaneous touches showed the hand of a master.

Meanwhile, Don Benito put up with it all like any other gentleman resigned to being fussed over by his barber. At least he was much more relaxed than he had been while being shaved. Indeed, he sat so pale and rigid now that Babo seemed like a Nubian sculptor finishing off a white statue-head.

All was over at last. The flag of Spain was removed, bundled up and tossed back into the flag-locker. Babo's warm breath blew away any stray hair which might have lodged down his master's back. Collar and cravat were readjusted. A speck of fluff was whisked off the velvet lapel.

When all this had been done, the servant backed off a little. He surveyed his master for a moment with an expression of quiet self-satisfaction, as if he had just created that figure with his own tasteful hands.

Captain Delano playfully complimented him on his achievement. At the same time, he congratulated Don Benito.

But nothing seemed to please the Spaniard — not sweet waters, nor shampooing, nor the loyalty of such a servant, nor Captain Delano's attempts to be sociable. Don Benito just went on sitting where he was and seemed to have sunk back into gloom.

Captain Delano presumed that his presence was no longer welcome. He made an excuse of wishing to see whether there were any signs of the breeze he had predicted, and left.

Chapter 9
Lunch in the Cabin

Captain Delano walked forward to the main-mast and stood there awhile thinking over the scene that had just taken place. He felt a sense of uneasiness return without being able to define quite why. A noise near the cuddy distracted him. When he turned round, he saw the servant holding his hand to his cheek. Captain Delano hurried towards him. There was blood on the man's face. Captain Delano was about to ask what had happened when Babo told him in a wailing voice.

'Ah, when will master get better from his sickness? It is only because the sour sickness breeds in him a sour heart that he treats Babo so. Cutting Babo with the razor because, only by accident, Babo had given his master one little scratch. And for the first time in so many days too. Ah, ah, ah,' he cried, holding his hand to his face.

Captain Delano could scarcely believe it. Was that why Don Benito by his sullen manner had forced him to leave? So that he could wreak his Spanish spite against this poor friend in private? What ugly passions this slavery produced in man. A surge of sympathy went out to the servant.

But before he could speak, the man had turned and was re-entering the cuddy, timidly and reluctantly.

Shortly afterwards, master and man emerged together. Don Benito was leaning on his servant as if nothing had happened.

Captain Delano was relieved. It was just a sort of love-quarrel after all, he thought.

He greeted Don Benito, and they slowly walked together on deck. They had gone only a few paces when the steward approached them. He was a tall mulatto who looked somewhat like an Indian prince, perhaps because of the pagoda-shaped turban he wore, made up of three or four cotton handkerchiefs wound about his head, tier on tier. He made a salaam and announced that lunch was ready in the cabin.

He proceeded to lead the way there, turning as he went with continual smiles and bows to draw them on. This display of elegant manners made small bare-headed Babo look quite insignificant.

Perhaps aware of his own inferiority, the servant eyed the graceful steward suspiciously. Though there could have been another reason why Babo watched the mulatto so jealously, Captain Delano thought. It could have been the result of the feeling which all full-blooded Africans have for people of mixed race.

As for the steward, perhaps his manner was not very dignified and perhaps it did not show much sense of self-respect. But it did indicate his extreme eagerness to please. That was something that Captain Delano found both Christian-like and praiseworthy.

He observed with interest that while the mulatto's complexion showed his mixed blood, his features were entirely European. Indeed, he had the face of a classical Greek statue.

'Don Benito,' he whispered, 'I am glad to see this usher of yours. The sight of him gives the lie to an ugly remark a Barbados planter once made to me. He said that when a mulatto has a regular European face, then watch out for him, he is a devil. But see, your steward here has features more regular than King George's of England, and yet there he nods and bows and smiles. He is a king indeed, the king of kind hearts and polite fellows. And what a pleasant voice he has too, don't you think?'

'He has, Señor.'

'But tell me, hasn't he always proved himself to be a good worthy fellow during the time you have known him?' asked Captain Delano. He paused while with a final bend of the knee the steward disappeared into the cabin. 'Come, I am curious to know for the reason just mentioned.'

'Francesco is a good man,' responded Don Benito rather sluggishly like a cool judge who wishes neither to find fault nor to flatter.

'Ah, I thought so. It would be strange indeed, and not very creditable to us whites, if what my Barbados planter said were true. A little of our blood mixed with the African's should improve the quality, and not have the effect of pouring vitriolic acid into black broth. It should not just improve the colour but also the character.'

'Doubtless, Señor, doubtless, but' — here Don Benito glanced at Babo — 'quite apart from the Africans, I have heard your planter's remark applied to the children of Spanish and Indian unions in our provinces. But I know nothing about the matter,' he added listlessly.

They entered the cabin.

The lunch was a frugal one — some of Captain Delano's fresh fish and pumpkins, biscuit and salt beef, the reserved bottle of cider, and the *San Dominick*'s last bottle of Canary wine.

As they entered, Francesco was hovering over the table with two or three mulatto assistants making the last adjustments. When they saw their master, they withdrew. Francesco bowed with a smile on his face, but his master did not deign to acknowledge him.

'I do not like to have more servants about me than I need,' he remarked to Captain Delano with an expression of distaste.

Host and guest sat down alone, like a childless married couple, at opposite ends of the table. Don Benito waved Captain Delano to his place, and weak though he was, he insisted that his guest be seated before he sat down himself.

Babo placed a rug under Don Benito's feet and a cushion behind his back. Then he positioned himself not behind his master's chair, but behind Captain Delano's. At first, this surprised Captain Delano. But it soon became evident that in placing himself there he was still being considerate to his master's wishes. By standing there, facing his master, he could the more readily anticipate his slightest need.

'This is an uncommonly intelligent fellow of yours, Don Benito,' whispered Captain Delano across the table.

'You say true, Señor.'

During the meal, Captain Delano's thoughts returned to parts of Don Benito's story, and he requested further details about some of the events.

'How was it,' he asked, 'that the scurvy and fever caused so much havoc among the sailors while destroying less than half of the slaves?'

This question seemed to call up before the Spaniard's eyes the whole scene of the plague, miserably reminding him of his solitude in a cabin where before he had had so many friends and officers round him. His hand shook, his face went pale, broken words escaped from his lips.

But then straightaway the horrors of those memories of the past seemed to be replaced by some insane terror of the present. He stared with crazed eyes before him, but there was nothing there — only the hand of his servant pushing the bottle of Canary wine over towards him. Eventually, a few sips helped partially to restore him. In response to Captain Delano's question, he made some vague reference to the different physical attributes of black and white people which enabled one to offer more resistance to certain illnesses than the other. It was an idea that Captain Delano had not heard of before.

After a while, Captain Delano thought it would be

appropriate to discuss with Don Benito something of the financial side of the business he had undertaken for him, especially regarding the new set of sails and other things of that sort. After all, Captain Delano was strictly accountable to his owners for all expenses. Naturally, he preferred to conduct such affairs in private and wanted the servant to leave. He was sure that Don Benito could manage without his attendant for a few moments. However, he did not suggest this, as he felt certain that as the conversation proceeded, Don Benito would realize without being prompted that it would be more proper to discuss such matters alone.

But this did not happen. So in the end, Captain Delano, catching Don Benito's eye and making a slight backward gesture with his thumb, whispered, 'Don Benito, pardon me, but there is something preventing me from speaking freely to you.'

At this, Don Benito's face changed. Captain Delano could only assume that the Spaniard resented the hint and saw in it some kind of slur against his servant. After a moment's pause, Don Benito assured Captain Delano that there was no reason why the servant should not remain. Since losing his officers, he had made Babo (whose original position, it now appeared, had been captain of the slaves) not only his constant attendant and companion, but also his confidant in all things.

After this, there was nothing more to be said. Though Captain Delano couldn't help feeling a little touch of irritation at not having been granted such a simple request — especially when he was undertaking to go to considerable lengths to help Don Benito. But he put it down to the Spaniard's peevish nature. He filled his glass and got on with the business.

The price of the sails and other matters was agreed upon. But while they were discussing it, Captain Delano observed a difference in Don Benito's attitude. His original offer of assistance had been hailed with wild excitement, but now that it was reduced to a business transaction, only in-difference and apathy were displayed. Don Benito, in fact, appeared to put up with hearing the details more out of regard to common politeness than from any impression that great benefits to himself and his voyage were involved.

Soon, his manner became still more reserved. Captain Delano gave up the effort of trying to draw him into social talk. The Spaniard, his bitter mood gnawing away at him, sat twitching his beard. He ignored the hand of his silent servant as he slowly pushed the bottle of Canary wine towards him.

When lunch was over, the two captains sat down on a cushioned bench, and the servant placed a pillow behind his master. The long continuance of the calm had by now affected the air. Don Benito sighed heavily as though for breath.

'Why don't you adjourn to the cuddy?' Captain Delano suggested. 'There is more air there.'

But Don Benito sat silent and motionless.

Meanwhile Babo knelt before him with a large fan of feathers. Francesco, coming in on tiptoe, handed the servant a little cup of aromatic waters with which at intervals he rubbed his master's brow. He smoothed the hair along the temples as a nurse does a child's. He didn't speak. He just rested his eye on his master's as though to refresh his spirit a little in the midst of his distress by this sight of silent loyalty.

Chapter 10
The Breeze

Presently, the ship's bell sounded two o'clock. And through the cabin windows could be detected the slight rippling of the sea. What was more, it came from the right direction.

'There,' exclaimed Captain Delano, 'I told you so, Don Benito. Look!'

He had risen to his feet and spoke with great excitement to try to rouse the Spaniard. But though the crimson curtain of the stern window near him that moment fluttered against his cheek, Don Benito seemed to welcome the breeze even less than he did the calm.

Poor man, Captain Delano thought. Bitter experience has taught him that one ripple does not make a wind, any more than one swallow makes a summer. But he is mistaken for once. I will get his ship in for him, and prove it.

'Do not disturb yourself, Don Benito,' he said. 'Remain here quietly and regain your strength. I myself will see how best to use this wind. It will give me pleasure to help in any way I can.'

When he gained the deck, Captain Delano started at the unexpected figure of Atufal. He was standing on the threshold to the cabin, fixed like a statue, like one of those sculptured door-keepers guarding the entrance to an

Egyptian tomb.

But this time the start was perhaps simply the result of coming upon the huge African so suddenly. There was nothing hostile or dangerous in Atufal's presence. He showed only a sullen submission. This was in contrast to the hatchet-polishers with their busy activity. Yet both said something about Don Benito's authority. It might have been lax, but whenever he chose to exert it, all men no matter how savage or colossal had to bow to it.

Captain Delano snatched a trumpet that hung from the bulwarks. He boldly advanced to the forward edge of the poop and began issuing his orders in his best Spanish. The few sailors and many slaves all seemed equally pleased and obediently set about heading the ship towards the harbour.

While giving some directions about setting a lower studding-sail, Captain Delano suddenly heard a voice faithfully repeating his orders. Turning, he saw Babo, now acting his original role as captain of the slaves. This assistance proved valuable. Tattered sails and warped yards were soon brought into some trim. The eager slaves pulled on ropes and tackle, chanting happy songs as they did so.

Good fellows, thought Captain Delano. With a little training they would make fine sailors. Why, even the women are pulling and singing. They must be some of those Ashanti women that I've heard make such excellent soldiers. But who's at the helm? I must have a good hand there.

He went to see.

The *San Dominick* was steered by a cumbrous tiller to which were attached large horizontal pulleys. At each pulley-end stood a subordinate black man. Between them, performing the responsible work at the tiller-head, was a Spanish seaman whose countenance showed that he shared in the general hopefulness and confidence at the coming of the breeze. He turned out to be the same man who had behaved with such a shame-faced air on the windlass.

'Ah, it is you, my man,' exclaimed Captain Delano. 'No more of that bashful look now, eh? Look straight forward and keep the ship so. You have a good hand I trust? And you want to get into harbour, don't you?'

The man assented with an inward chuckle and grasped the tiller-head firmly. At this, unnoticed by Captain Delano, the two Africans eyed the sailor intently.

Finding all well at the helm, Captain Delano went forward to the forecastle to see how things were going there.

The ship was now able to make way against the current. With the approach of evening, the breeze was sure to freshen.

Having done all that needed to be done for the present, Captain Delano gave his last orders to the sailors and turned aft to report matters to Don Benito in the cabin. Perhaps an additional motive for rejoining him was the hope of snatching a moment's private chat with him while the servant was busy on deck.

Beneath the poop, there were two approaches to the cabin from opposite sides. One was further forward than the other and therefore had a longer passage leading to the cabin. Making sure the servant was still on deck, Captain Delano took the nearest entrance, the one that was further forward, where Atufal still stood. He hurried on his way. When he arrived at the threshold to the cabin, he paused an instant so as to recover a little from his eagerness. Then, with the words of his intended business on his lips, he entered.

As he advanced towards the seated Spaniard, he heard another footstep keeping time with his own. From the opposite door, with a tray in his hand, the servant was likewise advancing.

'Confound the faithful fellow,' thought Captain Delano. 'What a tiresome coincidence.'

Possibly the irritation he felt might have been stronger but for the brisk confidence inspired by the breeze. But even so, he experienced a slight twinge as a sudden vague suspicion that Babo and Atufal were somehow in league with each other crossed his mind.

'Don Benito,' he said, 'I bring you good news. The breeze

will hold and will increase. By the way, your giant and time-keeper Atufal stands outside. By your order, of course?'

Don Benito recoiled. It was as though he sensed that he was being made fun of, but in such a skilful and polite way that there was nothing he could pick on to use as a retort.

He is like someone flayed alive, thought Captain Delano. It is impossible to touch him anywhere without causing him to flinch.

The servant moved across to his master and adjusted a cushion. Thus recalled to civility, Don Benito replied stiffly, 'You are right. The slave appears where you saw him according to my command. He has been instructed that if at the given hour I am below, he must take up his stand there and wait for me to come.'

'Come now. You must pardon me, but that is treating the poor fellow like an ex-king indeed. Ah, Don Benito,' Captain Delano continued, smiling, 'in spite of the freedom you allow in some things, I fear you are a bitter hard master at heart.'

Again, the Spaniard flinched. This time Captain Delano was sure it was from a genuine twinge of conscience.

Once more conversation became difficult. Captain Delano drew Don Benito's attention in vain to the now perceptible motion of the keel gently cleaving the sea. The Spaniard with a lack-lustre eye replied briefly and remotely.

The wind rose steadily and continued to blow right into the harbour. The *San Dominick* was borne swiftly along. As she rounded a point of land, the *Bachelor's Delight* came into full view in the distance.

Captain Delano went on deck and remained there for a while. He altered the ship's course so as to give the reef a wide berth and returned below for a few moments.

I will cheer my poor friend up this time, he thought.

'It gets better and better, Don Benito,' he cried as he cheerfully re-entered the cabin. 'Your cares will soon be at an end — at least for a while. You know how, when the anchor drops into the haven at the end of a long sad voyage, all its vast weight seems lifted from the captain's heart. We are getting on famously, Don Benito. My ship is in sight. Look through this side-light here. There she is, spruce and ship-shape. The *Bachelor's Delight*, my good friend. Ah, how this wind raises the spirits. Come, you must take a cup of coffee with me this evening. My old steward will give you as fine a cup as ever any sultan tasted. What do you say, Don Benito?'

At first, the Spaniard glanced feverishly up. He cast a longing look towards the *Bachelor's Delight* while his servant gazed into his face with silent concern. Suddenly his old coldness returned, and he dropped back against his cushions without speaking.

'Why don't you answer? Come, you have been my host all day. You wouldn't want hospitality to be all on one side, would you?'

'I cannot go,' was the response.

'What? It won't tire you. The ships will lie next to each other as near as they can without swinging foul. It will be little more than stepping from deck to deck. It will be like going from one room to another. Come, come, you mustn't refuse me.'

'I cannot go,' repeated Don Benito decisively and coldly.

He seemed to abandon all but the last vestiges of politeness. He sank into a kind of death-like sullenness. Biting his thin nails to the quick, he glanced — almost glared — at Captain Delano as if impatient that the presence of a stranger should prevent him from indulging his morbid humour to the full.

Meanwhile, the sound of the parted waters came in more gurglingly and merrily at the windows. It seemed to be reproaching Don Benito for his dark ill-temper. It seemed to be telling him that, no matter how much he sulked, even if he went mad with it, nature didn't care a bit. After all, he had only himself to blame.

But the foul mood was now at its depth, just as the fair wind was at its height.

Captain Delano, patient and good-natured though he was, could no longer endure it. There was something in Don Benito now that was far beyond any mere unsociability or sourness he had shown previously. Captain Delano was wholly at a loss to account for such behaviour. The combination of sickness with eccentricity, however extreme, was no excuse. He was sure there had been nothing in his own conduct to justify it.

The result was that Captain Delano's pride began to be roused. He himself became reserved. But it seemed to have no effect on Don Benito. Captain Delano therefore left him and went on deck once more.

The ship was now within less than two miles of the *Bachelor's Delight*. The whale-boat could be seen darting over the sea in between. Thanks to Captain Delano's skill as a pilot, it was not long before the two vessels lay anchored together like good neighbours.

Chapter 11
A Flash of Revelation

Before returning to his own vessel, Captain Delano had intended telling Don Benito further details of what he proposed to do to help him. But he was unwilling to place himself once more in a position where he could be rebuffed. He resolved therefore to leave the *San Dominick* immediately, now that he had seen her safely moored, without referring again to hospitality or business. He would make no plans about how to proceed. His future actions would be guided by future circumstances.

His boat was ready to take him on board, but Don Benito had not yet come on deck to see him depart.

Well, thought Captain Delano, if he has so little breeding, all the more reason why I should show him mine.

He descended to the cabin to bid a polite farewell, one that also perhaps contained an unspoken rebuke. But to his great satisfaction, Don Benito rose to his feet, supported by his servant. It was as though he was aware that Captain Delano was in a mild way returning the treatment that had been doled out to him. The Spaniard stood shakily and grasped Captain Delano's hand. He seemed to be too much agitated to speak.

But then, Don Benito's behaviour made Captain Delano

wonder whether he had been mistaken yet again. The Spaniard took on all his previous reserve and became even more depressed than before. With half-averted eyes, he reseated himself on the cushions without saying a word. Captain Delano too felt his own chilled feelings return. He bowed and withdrew.

He was hardly midway in the narrow corridor, dim as a tunnel, leading from the cabin to the stairs, when a sound fell on his ears. It was like the tolling for execution in some prison yard. In fact, it was the echo of the ship's flawed bell, striking the hour, drearily reverberating in this subterranean vault. It seemed to Captain Delano like an omen.

Instantly, with an impulse he could not restrain, his mind swarmed with superstitious suspicions. He paused. In images far swifter than these sentences, the minutest details of all his former distrusts swept through him.

Up till now, he had been too ready because of his trusting good-nature to argue away what had been reasonable fears. Why was Don Benito, so excessively polite at times, now quite unconcerned about common manners? Why did he not accompany his departing guest to the side of the ship? Did illness prevent him? But illness had not prevented him from more tiresome duties that day.

Captain Delano recalled the ambiguous way Don Benito had behaved a few moments before. The Spaniard had risen to his feet, grasped his guest's hand, motioned towards his hat. Then, in an instant, all had been eclipsed in sinister silence and gloom. It was as though Don Benito had repented for a brief moment, had decided at the final minute not to go ahead with some evil plot, and then had crushed all feelings of remorse. His last glance seemed to be sending Captain Delano to a disastrous fate — one that the Spaniard had no desire to prevent.

And why had Don Benito declined the invitation to visit the *Bachelor's Delight* that evening? Was it that he was less hardened than Judas who had been quite prepared to eat at the table of the person he meant to betray the same night?

What did all these enigmas and contraditions which Captain Delano had been puzzling over all day mean? They could only indicate that some secret attack was intended, couldn't they?

Atufal was at that moment lurking by the threshold outside — Atufal who was supposed to be a rebel and yet who obeyed orders like a punctual shadow. He was like a sentry standing at the entrance — perhaps more. Wasn't it Don Benito by his own confession who had stationed him there? Was the African now lying in wait?

The Spaniard was behind in his cabin. His slave was before at the entrance. To rush from darkness to light was the only and instinctive thing to do.

The next moment, with clenched jaw and hand, Captain Delano passed Atufal and stood unharmed on deck. He saw his trim ship lying peacefully at anchor and almost within call. He saw the whale-boat, with familiar faces in it, rising and falling on the short waves by the *San Dominick*'s side. Glancing about the decks where he stood, he saw the oakum-pickers still gravely plying their fingers, and he heard the low buzzing whistle and industrious hum of the hatchet-polishers, still busy at their endless occupation. He saw the chained figure of Atufal. He began to feel reassured.

But more than any of these things, he saw the healing kindness of nature around him, as the hazy sun shone mildly in the west and sank to its innocent sleep. His clenched jaw and hand relaxed.

Once again, he smiled at those fantasies that had mocked him. He even felt something like a tinge of remorse. How could he have harboured such thoughts even for a moment? By so doing, he had in effect betrayed his faith in the ever-watchful Providence above.

Captain Delano ordered the whale-boat to be hooked along to the gangway. During the few minutes it took for this to be done, a sort of saddened satisfaction stole over him as he thought of the kind acts he had performed that day for a stranger. After good deeds, he reflected, one's conscience is never ungrateful, even if the person who benefits may be.

At last, facing inward to the deck, he placed his foot on the first round of the side-ladder to begin his descent to the boat. At the same moment, he heard someone politely call his name. To his pleased surprise, he saw Don Benito advancing towards him. There was an air of unusual energy about him, as if at the last minute he meant to make amends for his recent rudeness.

With instinctive good feeling, Captain Delano withdrew his foot. He turned and went to meet him. As he did so, Don Benito's nervous eagerness increased, but his physical energy ran out. The servant, so as to support him better, placed his master's hand on his naked shoulder and gently held it there, making himself into a sort of crutch.

When the two captains reached one another, Don Benito again fervently took Captain Delano's hand. At the same time, he looked earnestly into his eyes. But, as before, he was too much overcome to speak.

I have done him wrong, Captain Delano reproached himself. I have been deceived by his apparent coldness. He has not meant to offend me in anything he has done.

Meanwhile, the servant, as though afraid that if the scene went on it might upset his master too much, seemed anxious to bring it to an end. And so, acting still as a crutch, and walking between the two captains, he advanced with them towards the gangway. But Don Benito would not let go Captain Delano's hand. As though full of remorse, he kept it in his grasp across the servant's body.

Soon they were standing by the side, looking over into the boat whose crew gazed upwards with curiosity. Waiting a moment for Don Benito to let go his hand, Captain Delano, who was now feeling rather embarrassed, lifted his foot to step over the threshold of the open gangway. But still Don Benito would not relinquish his hand.

Then, in an agitated voice, Don Benito said, 'I can go no further. I must bid you goodbye here. Goodbye, my dear dear Don Amasa. Go — go!' He suddenly tore his hand free.

'Go, and God guard you better than me, my best friend.'

Captain Delano was moved by these words, and he would now have stayed a little longer. But then he caught the eye of the servant who seemed to be humbly reproving him. With a hasty farewell, he descended into his boat, followed by the continual goodbyes of Don Benito who remained rooted in the gangway.

Captain Delano seated himself in the stern, and making a last salute, ordered the boat to be shoved off. The crew had their oars on end. The bowsmen pushed the boat out far enough for the oars to be dropped lengthwise.

The instant that was done, Don Benito sprang over the bulwarks and fell at Captain Delano's feet. At the same time, he called towards his ship, but his words were so frenzied that no one in the boat could understand him.

But others apparently did. Three sailors from three different and distant parts of the ship splashed into the sea and began swimming towards the boat as if with the intention of rescuing their captain.

The officer in charge of the boat was disconcerted. 'What's going on?' he asked urgently.

Turning a disdainful smile on the eccentric Spaniard, Captain Delano answered, 'I don't know, and I'm past caring. It seems as if Don Benito here has taken it into his head to give his people the impression that we are trying to kidnap him. Or else —'

He broke off, starting at the chattering hubbub in the ship, above which rang the alarm-signal of the hatchet-polishers. He gave a wild cry. 'Give way for your lives.' He seized Don Benito by the throat. 'This plotting pirate means murder!'

Here, as though demonstrating the truth of his words, Babo was seen on the rail overhead with a dagger in his hand. He was poised in the act of leaping, as if with a desperate loyalty, he meant to befriend his master to the last.

At the same time, seemingly in support of the servant, the

three white sailors were trying to clamber into the bow of the boat.

Meanwhile, the whole crowd of Africans, as though infuriated at the sight of their captain in danger, hung threateningly in one black avalanche over the bulwarks.

All of this, as well as what went before and what followed, occurred with such confusion and speed, that past, present and future seemed blurred in one.

Seeing Babo coming, Captain Delano had flung Don Benito aside, almost in the very act of seizing him. He was automatically thrown back with his arms raised, so that he was able quickly to grapple with the servant as he landed. Indeed, in the positions in which they found themselves, with the dagger aimed at Captain Delano's heart, it looked as though Captain Delano was the object of the man's attack. But the weapon was wrenched away, and the assailant was dashed down into the bottom of the boat. The disentangled oars were soon at work, and the boat began to speed through the sea.

At this point, Captain Delano on one side again clutched the half falled Don Benito with his left hand, regardless of the fact that the Spaniard had fainted. On the other side, he held the prostrate African down with his right foot. His right arm was pressed for added speed on the after oar. He gazed forward and encouraged his men to their utmost.

The officer in charge of the boat had at last succeeded in beating off the sailors who were hanging onto the sides. He was turning aft to assist the bowsman at his oar when he suddenly called out to Captain Delano, 'Watch out there.'

At the same moment, a Portuguese oarsman shouted to him, 'Listen to what the Spaniard is saying.'

Glancing down at his feet, Captain Delano saw the freed hand of the servant holding a second dagger. It was a small one which he had had concealed in the wool of his hair. With this, he was writhing up from the bottom of the boat like a snake. He was aiming the dagger at his master's heart.

His face was livid with revenge, revealing the concentrated purpose of his soul.

The Spaniard, half-choked, was vainly shrinking away. Husky words fell from his lips, incoherent to all but the Portuguese.

It was then that a flash of revelation swept across Captain Delano's mind, a mind that had for so long been blind. With a sudden clearness, the whole mysterious behaviour of Don Benito was explained, together with every puzzling event of the day and the entire past voyage of the *San Dominick*.

He struck down Babo's hand, but his own heart struck him harder. With infinite pity, he withdrew his hold from Don Benito.

It wasn't Captain Delano that the African had intended to stab by leaping into the boat. It was Don Benito.

Chapter 12
The Fight for the *San Dominick*

Both the African's hands were held. Glancing up towards the *San Dominick*, Captain Delano, now that the scales had dropped from his eyes, saw the Africans for what they were. They were not an ill-disciplined mob, not an excited crowd, not frantically concerned for Don Benito. Their mask had been torn away, and they were revealed, flourishing hatchets and knives in ferocious piratical revolt. Like delirious dervishes, the six Ashantis danced on the poop. Prevented by their enemies from springing into the water, the Spanish boys were hurrying up to the topmost spars. Those few Spanish sailors who had been less alert and not jumped overboard could be seen on deck helplessly lost amongst the Africans.

Captain Delano hailed his own vessel. He ordered the ports to be raised and the guns run out. But before this could be done, the cable of the *San Dominick* had been cut. The frayed end lashed out and whipped away the canvas shroud about the beak. As the bleached hull swung round towards the open sea, the figure-head was suddenly revealed. It was death in the form of a human skeleton. The chalky bones were a comment on the chalked words below, 'Follow your leader'.

At the sight, Don Benito covered his face and wailed out, 'It is Aranda, my murdered unburied friend.'

When they reached the *Bachelor's Delight*, Captain Delano called for ropes. The African was tied up and hoisted to the deck. He made no resistance.

Next, Captain Delano tried to assist the now almost helpless Don Benito up the side. But the Spaniard, weak though he was, refused to move or be moved until the African had been put below and was no longer in view. Only when he was at last assured that this had been done did he agree to go on board.

The boat was immediately sent back to pick up the three sailors in the water. The guns were made ready, but because the *San Dominick* had drifted somewhat astern of the *Bachelor's Delight*, only the aftermost gun could be brought to bear. This they fired six times. The intention was to cripple the fleeing ship by bringing down her spars. But only a few unimportant ropes were shot away.

Soon the ship was beyond the gun's range, moving away out of the bay. The Africans could be seen clustered round the bow-sprit. One moment they hurled taunting cries at their adversaries, the next they hailed the now darkening expanses of the ocean with upthrown arms. They were like cawing crows who had escaped from the hand of the fowler.

The first impulse was to slip the cables and give chase. But on second thoughts it seemed likely they would have more success if they used the small boats — the whale-boat and the yawl.

Captain Delano asked Don Benito what fire-arms they had on board the *San Dominick*.

'None that can be used,' Don Benito told him. 'In the earlier stages of the mutiny, one of the cabin-passengers who died soon after broke the locks of the few muskets that were on board.'

Don Benito went on with all his remaining strength. 'I entreat you, do not give chase with either ship or boat. The Africans have already proved themselves to be desperate men. If you try to board the ship, it will result in nothing but a total massacre of the sailors still left on board.'

But Captain Delano disregarded this warning. It came, he felt, from a man whose spirit had been crushed by misery. He determined to go ahead with his plan.

The boats were got ready and armed. Captain Delano ordered his men into them. He was about to join them when Don Benito grasped his arm.

'Do not go,' he cried. 'You have saved my life, Señor. You cannot now throw away your own.'

The officers also made strong objections to their commander's going. They felt it would not be in their interests or in those of the voyage. Captain Delano too had a duty to the owners to remain on board the *Bachelor's Delight*.

Weighing up these arguments a moment, Captain Delano came to the conclusion that he had to stay. He appointed his chief mate to head the party. He was a strong and active man and had once served on a privateer. So as to encourage the sailors the more, they were told that the Spanish captain considered his ship as good as lost. The ship and her cargo, including some gold and silver, were worth more than a thousand doubloons. If the sailors captured her, then a fair share of that money would be theirs. This news was greeted by an enthusiastic cheer.

The fugitives in the *San Dominick* had now almost reached the open sea. It was nearly night, but the moon was rising. After long hard pulling, the boats approached the ship's stern.

At a suitable distance, the men lay down their oars in order to fire their muskets. Having no bullets to return, the Africans sent their yells. But after a second volley, they hurled their hatchets like Red Indians. One hatchet took off a sailor's fingers. Another struck the whale-boat's bow, cutting off a rope there and sticking in the gunwale like a woodman's axe. The mate snatched it up, quivering from where it had embedded itself, and hurled it back. It stuck in the ship's broken quarter-gallery and remained there.

Because of the Africans' hot reception, the crew kept a more respectful distance. They hovered just out of reach of the hurling hatchets. They knew that a hand-to-hand battle was inevitable. Their plan was to trick the Africans into disarming themselves of their most murderous weapons by foolishly flinging them as missiles short of their mark into the sea. But before long, the Africans realized what was going on and stopped throwing hatchets. Those who had lost their weapons replaced them with hand-spikes. This was what Captain Delano's men had hoped would happen, and these new weapons proved to be less effective when it came to the later struggle.

Meanwhile, because of a strong wind, the ship still cut through the water. The boats alternately fell behind or pulled up to her in order to discharge fresh volleys.

The fire was mostly directed towards the stern since that was where the Africans were mainly clustered. But the object was not to kill or maim them. The object was to capture them with the ship. To do this, the ship had to be boarded, but they couldn't accomplish this from the boats while the ship was sailing so fast.

The mate, observing the Spanish boys still aloft as high as they could get, had an idea. He called to them to descend to the yards and cut the sails adrift. This the boys did.

It was about this time that two Spaniards dressed as sailors who showed themselves conspicuously were killed, not by volleys but by deliberate marksman's shots. How this came about is made clear later.

It also appeared afterwards that Atufal and the Spaniard at the helm were killed by one of the general discharges. The result was, with the loss of sails and the loss of leaders, the Africans were unable to manage the ship.

With creaking masts, the *San Dominick* came heavily round to the wind. The prow slowly swung round so that it was visible to the men in the boats, its skeleton gleaming in the horizontal moonlight, and casting a gigantic ribbed shadow upon the water. One extended arm of the ghostly figure seemed to be beckoning to the men in the small boats to avenge it.

The boats closed in, one on each bow.

'Follow your leader!' the mate cried, and the men began to board the ship. Sealing-spears and cutlasses crossed hatchets and hand-spikes. The African women, huddled on the long-boat amidships, raised a wailing chant to which the clash of steel acted as a chorus.

For a time, the attack wavered. The Africans formed themselves into a wedge to beat it back. The sailors were almost repelled. They had as yet been unable to gain a footing. They fought like troopers in the saddle, with one leg flung sideways over the bulwarks and the other dangling over the edge, wielding their cutlasses like carters' whips. But they could not advance. In fact, they were almost driven backwards.

Then they reformed themselves to present a united front and with an exultant roar they sprang inboard. There they became entangled with the Africans and separated again. For the space of a few moments, there was a vague muffled inner sound — like that made by a submerged sword-fish rushing here and there through shoals of black-fish. Soon the white faces came to the surface. They reunited in a band and were joined by the Spanish seamen. Irresistibly, they drove the Africans back towards the stern.

But a barricade of casks and sacks had been thrown up by the main-mast from one side of the ship to the other. Here the Africans turned to face their assailants. They scorned to make peace or call a truce, though they were in need of time to recuperate. But the tireless sailors didn't pause. They leaped over the barricade and again closed with the Africans.

The Africans were now exhausted and fought with despair. Their red tongues lolled wolf-like from their mouths. But the sailors set their teeth with determination. Not a word was spoken. In five minutes, the ship was won.

Nearly a score of the Africans had been killed. Some had

been killed by the musket fire. Others had been hacked and mangled by the long-edged sealing-spears, their deep-cut wounds resembling those inflicted by the poled scythes of the Highlanders used on the English at Preston Pans.

On the other side, no one had been killed, though several were wounded, some severely, including the mate. The surviving Africans were temporarily made safe. The ship was towed back into harbour, and at midnight she once more lay at anchor.

Two days were spent in refitting, and then the ships sailed together for Conception in Chile. They then proceeded to Lime in Peru where the whole affair from the very beginning was investigated before the vice-regal courts.

Midway on the voyage, the ill-fated Don Benito, set free from his dreadful ordeal, showed some signs of regaining his health. But as he himself predicted, shortly before arriving at Lima, he suffered a relapse. He finally became so weak that he had to be carried ashore.

Hearing of his story and his plight, one of the many religious institutions of the city opened its doors to him and gave him refuge. There he was looked after by both doctors and priests. One member of the order volunteered to be his special nurse to watch over him night and day.

Chapter 13
Don Benito's Statement

The following extracts are translated from one of the official Spanish documents. It is hoped that it will shed light on what has been written so far. It also reveals the true port of departure of the *San Dominick* and the true history of her voyage down to the time when she touched at the island of St Maria.

But before proceeding with the extracts, it may be as well to preface them with a comment.

The document selected from among many others for partial translation contains the sworn statement made by Don Benito, the first to be taken in the case. It was felt at the time for both legal and natural reasons that some of the events described were unbelievable. The court was inclined to think that Don Benito, having had his mind disturbed by what he had been through, raved about things which could never have happened.

But the subsequent statements of the surviving sailors supported what their captain said in some of the most unusual details and so gave credibility to the rest. Without this confirmation, the court would have considered it its duty to reject Don Benito's statement. But having this confirmation, in its final decision, it based its capital sentences on it.

I, DON JOSÉ DE ABOS AND PADILLA, His Majesty's Notary for the Royal Revenue, and Registrar of this Province, and Public Notary of the Holy Crusade of this Bishopric, etc.

Do certify and declare as is required by law, that in the criminal case commenced on the twenty-fourth of the month of September in the year seventeen hundred and ninety-nine, against the negroes of the ship *San Dominick*, the following statement was made before me:

Statement of the first witness, DON BENITO CERENO

The same day and month and year, His Honour, Doctor Juan Martinez de Rozas, Councillor of the Royal Audience of this Kingdom, and learned in the law of this State, ordered the captain of the ship *San Dominick* to appear. This he did, in his litter, attended by the monk Infelez. He received the oath from the monk and swore by God, our Lord, and made the sign of the Cross. Under this oath, he promised to tell the truth regarding everything he knew and should be asked.

On being questioned, according to the correct procedure, he said that on the twentieth of May last, he set sail with his ship from the port of Valparaiso, bound for Callao. His cargo consisted of produce of the country as well as thirty cases of hardware and one hundred and sixty blacks of both sexes, mostly belonging to Don Alexandro Aranda, gentleman, of the city of Mendoza. The crew of the ship consisted of thirty-six men, besides the persons who went as passengers. The negroes were in part as follows.

Here, in the original follows a list of some fifty names, descriptions and ages, compiled from certain recovered documents of Aranda's and also from recollections of the witness. Only portions of this are extracted here.

. . . One, from about eighteen to nineteen years, named

95

José. This was the man that waited on his master, Don Alexandro. He speaks Spanish well, having served his master four or five years.

. . . A mulatto, named Francesco, the cabin steward. He has a good appearance and voice, having sung in the Valparaiso churches. He is a native of the province of Buenos Ayres and is aged about thirty-five years.

. . . A clever negro named Dago who had been for many years a grave-digger among the Spaniards, aged forty-six years.

. . . Four old negroes, born in Africa, aged from sixty to seventy, but healthy. They were calkers by trade. Their names are as follows — the first was named Muri, and he was killed (as also was his son named Diamelo); the second, Nacta; the third, Yola, likewise killed; the fourth, Ghofan.

. . . Six full-grown negroes, aged from thirty to forty-five, all untrained and born among the Ashantis — Martinqui, Yan, Lecbe, Mapenda, Yambaio, Akim — four of whom were killed.

. . . A powerful negro named Atufal. He was supposed to have been a chief in Africa. Because of this, his owner set great store by him.

. . . A small negro from Senegal who had lived some years among the Spaniards. He was aged about thirty, and his name was Babo.

. . . That he does not remember the names of the others. But he still expects the rest of Don Alexandro's papers will be found which give full details of the slaves. These he will place before the court.

. . . And thirty-nine women and children of all ages.

[*The catalogue over, the statement goes on.*]

. . . That all the negroes slept upon deck, as is usual in this kind of transportation, and none of them wore fetters. This was because the owner, his friend Aranda, told him that they were all well-behaved.

. . . That on the seventh night after leaving port, at three o'clock in the morning, the negroes suddenly revolted. All the Spaniards were asleep except the two officers who were on watch. These were the boatswain, Juan Robles, and the carpenter, Juan Bautista Gayete, and the helmsman and his boy. The negroes severely wounded the boatswain and the carpenter, and went on to kill eighteen of those men who were sleeping on deck, some with hand-spikes and hatchets, and others by tying them up and throwing them overboard alive.

. . . That they left about seven of the Spaniards on deck, as he thinks, alive and tied, to manoeuvre the ship. Three or four more who hid themselves also remained alive. Although the negroes in their revolt succeeded in making themselves masters of the hatchway, six or seven Spaniards escaped through into the cockpit without being prevented by them.

. . . That during the act of revolt, the mate and another person, whose name he does not recollect, attempted to come up through the hatchway. But they were quickly wounded and had to return to the cabin.

. . . That the witness resolved at break of day to come up the companion-way where the negro Babo was. He was the ringleader. Atufal who assisted him was also there. The witness spoke to them and urged them to cease committing such atrocities. At the same time, he asked them what they wanted and what they intended to do. He himself offered to obey whatever they commanded. In spite of this, in his presence they threw three men overboard, tied up and alive.

. . . That they told the witness to come up on deck, promising that they would not kill him. The witness did this, and the negro Babo asked him whether there were any negro countries in those seas that they might be taken to. The witness answered that there were none.

. . . That the negro Babo afterwards told him to take them to Senegal or to the neighbouring islands of St Nicholas. And he answered that this was impossible for a number of reasons — the great distance involved, the necessity of rounding Cape Horn, the bad condition of the vessel, the lack of provisions, sails and water. But the negro Babo replied that he had to take them, and that the negroes would follow everything the witness required as far as eating and drinking were concerned.

. . . That after a long conference, the witness agreed to take the negroes to Senegal. He was forced to agree because the negroes threatened to kill all the whites if he refused. He told them that the thing he most needed for the voyage was water. That they would have to go near the coast in order to take it on board. Then after that, they would proceed on their course.

. . . That the negro Babo agreed to this. The witness steered towards the intermediary ports in the hope of meeting some Spanish or foreign vessel that would save them.

. . . That within ten or eleven days they sighted land and continued their course by it in the vicinity of Nasca.

. . . That the witness observed that the negroes were now restless and mutinous because he did not make any attempt to take in water.

. . . That the negro Babo insisted with threats that it should be done without fail the following day.

. . . That the witness told the negro Babo that the place was unsuitable. Plainly the coast was steep, and the rivers marked on the maps were not to be found, together with other reasons appropriate to the time and circumstances. That the best way would be to go to the island of Santa Maria which was an uninhabited island where they might water easily as foreign ships did.

. . . That the witness did not go to Pisco which was near, nor make any other port along that coast. Because the negro Babo had warned him several times that he would kill all the whites if the witness approached any city, town or settlement of any kind along the coast along which they were sailing.

. . . That the witness immediately changed his course,

steering for Santa Maria. His hope was that on the voyage or near the island, he might be able to find a vessel that would help him. Or alternatively, he could escape from the ship in a boat and make for the nearby coast of Arruco.

. . . That the negroes Babo and Atufal held daily conferences in which they discussed what was necessary for their plan of returning to Senegal. They talked about whether they should kill all the Spaniards and particularly the witness.

. . . That eight days after leaving the coast of Nasca, the witness was on watch a little after day-break when the negro Babo, soon after his meeting with Atufal, came to where he was. The negro Babo told him that he was determined to kill his master, Don Alexandro Aranda. He gave two reasons for this. The first was that he and his companions could not otherwise be sure of their liberty. The other was that in order to keep the seamen in a state of subjugation, he wanted to prepare a warning of what would happen to them if any of them tried to oppose him. This warning could be presented most powerfully by means of the death of Don Alexandro. What this meant the witness did not at the time understand, other than that the death of Don Alexandro was intended.

. . . That moreover the negro Babo told the witness, before the deed was committed, to call the mate, Raneds, who was sleeping in the cabin. As the witness understood it, this was because the negro Babo feared lest the mate, who was a good navigator, should be killed with Don Alexandro and the rest.

. . . That the witness, who had been a friend of Don Alexandro's since they were boys, appealed to the negro Babo and begged him not to do this thing. But in vain. The negro Babo told him that it could not be prevented, and that all the Spaniards risked death if they attempted to stop him doing this, or anything else.

. . . That the witness, giving up the struggle, called the mate, Raneds, who was kept to one side. Immediately, the negro Babo commanded the Ashanti Martinqui and the Ashanti Lecbe to go and commit the murder.

. . . That those two went down with hatchets to the berth of Don Alexandro.

. . . That, yet half alive and mangled, they dragged him on deck.

. . . That they were going to throw him overboard in that state, but the negro Babo stopped them. He ordered that the murder be completed on the deck in front of him. When this was done, he gave instructions that the body should be carried below, forward.

. . . That nothing more was seen of it by the witness for three days.

. . . That Don Alonzo Sidonia, an old man, long resident at Valparaiso, who was travelling on the ship in order to take up a civil post in Peru to which he had recently been appointed, was at the time sleeping in the berth opposite Don Alexandro's. He was awakened by Don Alexandro's cries. Terrified by the sight of the negroes with their bloody hatchets in their hands, he threw himself into the sea through a window that was near him and drowned. The witness had no power to assist him or rescue him from the sea.

. . . That a short time after Aranda had been killed, the other passengers were brought upon deck. These were Don Francisco Masa of Mendoza who was middle-aged and a cousin of Don Alexandro's, and the young Don Joaquin, Marques de Aramboalaza who had recently come from Spain, with his Spanish servant Ponce, and Aranda's three young clerks — José Mozairi, Lorenzo Bargas and Hermenegildo Gandix — all from Cadiz.

. . . That the negroes kept Don Joaquin and Hermenegildo Gandix alive for reasons that were to become apparent later. But the negro Babo ordered Don Francisco Masa, José Mozairi and Lorenzo Borgas with Ponce the servant to be thrown alive into the sea, together with the boatswain, Juan Robles, the boatswain's mates, Manuel Viscaya and

Roderigo Hurta, and four of the sailors. They made no resistance, nor did they beg for anything except mercy.

. . . That the boatswain, Juan Robles, who knew how to swim, kept the longest above water. He prayed as long as he was able, and with the last words he uttered, he charged the witness to have a mass said to Our Lady of Succour for his soul.

. . . That during the three days that followed, the witness was uncertain what fate had befallen the remains of Don Alexandro. He frequently asked the negro Babo where they were, and if they were still on board, whether they were to be preserved for burial ashore. He entreated that orders be given for this to be done.

. . . That the negro Babo answered nothing till the fourth day. Then, at sunrise, when the witness came on deck, the negro Babo showed him a skeleton which had been put in the place of the ship's proper figure-head — the image of Christopher Columbus, the discoverer of the New World.

. . . That the negro Babo asked him if he knew whose skeleton that was, and whether from its whiteness he should not think it likely to be a white man's.

. . . That the negro Babo, pulling back the hands with which the witness tried to cover his face, came close and pointing to the prow said words to this effect: 'Keep faith with the blacks from here to Senegal, or you shall in spirit, as now in body, follow your leader.'

. . . That the same morning, the negro Babo took each Spaniard forward in succession, and asked him whose skeleton that was, and whether from its whiteness he should not think it likely to be a white man's.

. . . That each Spaniard covered his face, and to each the negro repeated the words which he had said in the first place to the witness.

. . . That they (the Spaniards) were then assembled aft, and the negro Babo addressed them fiercely. He had now done all, he said. He told the witness (as navigator for the negroes) that he could continue his course. He warned him and all of them that they would, soul and body, go the same way as Don Alexandro if he saw them (the Spaniards) speak or plot anything against them (the negroes). This threat was repeated every day.

. . . That before the events last mentioned, they had tied up the cook to throw him overboard because of something they heard him speak — it is not known what. But finally, the negro Babo spared his life at the request of the witness.

. . . That the witness made every effort to preserve the lives of the remaining whites. He tried to speak peacefully and calmly to the negroes. A few days later, he agreed to draw up a document in which he bound himself to carry the negroes to Senegal, and they bound themselves not to kill any more Spaniards. This was signed by the witness and those sailors who could write. The negro Babo signed on behalf of himself and all the blacks. The document stated further that the witness formally made over the ship to the negroes, together with the cargo. This for the time satisfied them and quieted them.

. . . But the next day, the more surely to guard against the sailors escaping, the negro Babo commanded all the boats to be destroyed — all except the long-boat which was un-seaworthy, and the cutter in good condition which he had lowered down into the hold as he knew it would be wanted for towing the water casks.

[*There follow particulars of the prolonged and bewildering navigation that came after, together with incidents of a disastrous calm. One passage from this portion of the statement is given here, namely:*]

. . . That on the fifth day of the calm, the negroes became irritable. All on board had been suffering much from the heat and from lack of water. Five had gone mad and died in fits. But then, on that day, they killed Raneds, the mate. It was because of a chance gesture the mate made to the witness in the act of handing over a quadrant. The negroes considered the gesture suspicious though it was in fact harmless. For this act, they were afterwards sorry. The mate was the only remaining navigator on board, except for the witness.

... That omitting other events which happened daily and which can only serve uselessly to recall past misfortunes and conflicts, they at last arrived at the island of Santa Maria. It had taken them seventy-three days, reckoned from the time they sailed from Nasca. During this period, they had but a scanty allowance of water and were afflicted with the calms before mentioned. They arrived at Santa Maria on the seventeenth of the month of August at about six o'clock in the afternoon and cast anchor, without knowing it, very near the American ship, the *Bachelor's Delight*, commanded by the generous Captain Amasa Delano, which lay in the same bay. But at six o'clock next morning, when the negroes saw the port and the ship at a distance which they had not expected to see there, they became uneasy.

... That the negro Babo pacified them and assured them that they need not have any fear.

... That, straightaway, he ordered the figure on the bow to be covered with canvas, as if for repairs, and had the decks a little set to order.

... That for a time, the negro Babo and the negro Atufal conferred.

... That the negro Atufal was for sailing away, but the negro Babo would not. Instead, he set about working on a plan of his own.

... That at last, he came to the witness and told him to say and do all the things that the witness claims to have said and done to the American captain.

... That the negro Babo gave him a solemn warning. He was not to vary in the least from what he had been told. He was not to utter a word or give a look that would reveal the truth about past events or the present state of the ship. If he did so, he would be killed instantly, together with all his companions. The negro Babo showed him a dagger which

103

he carried on his person. He said something to the effect, as he understood it, that that dagger would be as alert as his eye.

. . . That the negro Babo then announced his plan to the other blacks who were pleased with it.

. . . That he then, in order to disguise the truth, devised many stratagems, in some of which the need to deceive and the need to have a form of defence were combined. An example of this was the way the six Ashantis, before named, who were his henchmen, were deployed. He stationed them on the break of the poop, as if to clean certain hatchets (in cases, which were part of the cargo). But in reality, they were to use the hatchets and distribute them as needed, whenever the negro Babo gave the word.

. . . That among other schemes the negro Babo thought up was the device of presenting Atufal, his right-hand man, as a figure in chains — though in a moment, the chains could be thrown off.

. . . That the negro Babo informed the witness in every detail how he was expected to behave in every part of his plan, and what story he was to tell on every occasion. He repeatedly threatened him with death if he varied in the slightest detail.

. . . That the negro Babo was aware that many of the negroes would be difficult to control. He therefore appointed the four aged negroes, who were calkers, to keep what order they could among them on the decks.

. . . That the negro Babo again and again addressed the Spaniards and his fellow blacks, telling them about what he intended, about the stratagems he had set up, and about the invented story that the witness was to tell. He warned them that none of them must vary from the story.

. . . That these arrangements were made and matured during the interval of two or three hours between their first sighting the ship and the arrival on board of Captain Amasa Delano.

. . . That this happened about half-past seven o'clock in

the morning. Captain Amasa Delano came in his boat, and everyone received him gladly.

... That the witness forced himself, as well as he could, to act the part of principal owner and free captain of the ship. He told Captain Amasa Delano, when asked, that he came from Buenos Ayres and was bound for Lima with three hundred negroes. That off Cape Horn and in a subsequent fever, many negroes had died. That also, in a similar way, all the sea officers and most of the crew had died.

[And so the statement goes on, recounting in detail the invented story which Babo dictated to the witness and which was imposed through the witness on Captain Delano. It also recounts the friendly offers of help made by Captain Delano, together with other things, but these are all omitted here. After the invented story, etc., the statement continues:]

... That the generous Captain Amasa Delano remained on board all the day till he left the ship anchored at six o'clock in the evening.

... That the witness spoke to him always of his pretended misfortunes according to the circumstances already mentioned.

... That he did not have the opportunity to say a single word or give him the least hint of the true state of affairs.

... That this was because the negro Babo played the part of an officious servant with every appearance of being submissive and being nothing but a humble slave.

... That the negro Babo did not leave the witness for a single moment so that he could observe the witness's actions and words, for the negro Babo understands Spanish well.

... That there were, in any case, others always close at hand constantly on the watch who similarly understood Spanish.

... That on one occasion, while the witness was standing on deck conversing with Amasa Delano, the negro Babo made a secret sign and drew him (the witness) aside.

. . . That he made it seem as though the witness himself had decided on this.

. . . That then, having been drawn aside, the negro Babo told the witness to gain full particulars from Amasa Delano about his ship, crew and arms.

. . . That the witness asked, 'What for?'

. . . That the negro Babo answered, 'Can't you guess?'

. . . That the witness was horrified at the thought of what might happen to the generous Captain Amasa Delano.

. . . That he at first refused to ask the desired questions and used every argument to try to persuade the negro Babo to give up his new plan.

. . . That the negro Babo showed him the point of his dagger.

. . . That after the information had been obtained, the negro Babo again drew him aside. He told him that that very night, he (the witness) would be captain of two ships instead of one. Because, with a great part of the American ship's crew absent fishing, the six Ashantis, without anyone else, would easily take it.

. . . That, at the same time, he said other things to the same purpose.

. . . That no entreaties could make him change his mind.

. . . That before Amasa Delano came on board, there had been no hint of intending the capture of the American ship.

. . . That the witness was powerless to prevent this plan.

. . . That in some things his memory is confused, and he cannot distinctly recall every event.

. . . That as soon as they had cast anchor at six o'clock in the evening, as has before been stated, the American captain took his leave to return to his own vessel.

. . . That on a sudden impulse, which the witness believes to have come from God and his angels, he followed the generous Captain Amasa Delano as far as the gunwale after the farewell had been said.

. . . That he stayed there under the pretence of taking leave until Amasa Delano was seated in his boat.

. . . That when the boat shoved off, the witness sprang from the gunwale into the boat.

. . . That he fell into the boat, he knows not how, except that God was protecting him.

. . . That —

[*Here, in the original, follows the account of what happened at the escape and how the* San Dominick *was retaken. The voyage to the coast is then described, including many expressions of 'eternal gratitude' to the 'generous Captain Amasa Delano'. The statement then repeats remarks made previously, and includes a partial recapitulation of the negroes, making a record of the individual parts they played in events. This was by command of the court in order to provide information on which the criminal sentences could be based. The following is from this portion of the statement:*]

. . . That he believes that all the negroes approved of the revolt when it was accomplished, though most of them did not know of the plan beforehand.

. . . That the negro José, who was eighteen years old and in the personal service of Don Alexandro, was the person who informed the negro Babo about the state of things in the cabin before the revolt.

. . . That this is known because he was seen several times by the mate.

. . . That before midnight, he used to come from his berth, which was under his master's in the cabin, to the deck where the ringleader and his associates were, and have secret conversations with the negro Babo.

. . . That one night, the mate had to drive him away twice.

. . . That this same negro José joined Lecbe and Martinqui in stabbing his master Don Alexandro after he had been dragged half-lifeless to the deck.

. . . That where Lecbe and Martinqui were commanded to do so by the negro Babo, José joined in voluntarily.

. . . That the mulatto steward Francesco was among the ringleaders of the revolt and was devoted to the negro Babo and ready to do anything for him.

. . . That in order to win the approval of the negro Babo, Francesco suggested, just before a meal in the cabin, poisoning a dish for the generous Captain Amasa Delano. This is known and believed because the negroes have spoken of it. But the negro Babo, who had something else planned, refused to allow Francesco to do it.

. . . That the Ashanti Lecbe was one of the worst of them.

. . . That on the day the ship was retaken, he assisted in her defence with a hatchet in each hand. With one of these, he wounded the chief mate of Amasa Delano in the chest as he first boarded the ship. Everyone knew this.

. . . That Lecbe struck Don Francisco Masa with a hatchet in the presence of the witness. This was when Lecbe was dragging him to throw him overboard alive by order of the negro Babo.

. . . That Lecbe also took part in the murder, already mentioned, of Don Alexandro and others of the cabin-passengers.

. . . That owing to the fury with which the Ashantis fought in the battle with the boats, only Lecbe and Yan survived.

. . . That Yan was as evil as Lecbe.

. . . That Yan was the man who by Babo's command willingly prepared the skeleton of Don Alexandro.

. . . That the negroes afterwards told the witness how this was done, but this is something he can never speak of so long as he wishes to remain sane.

. . . That Yan and Lecbe were the two who riveted the skeleton to the bow at night during a calm. This also the negroes told the witness.

. . . That the negro Babo was the person who traced the inscription below it.

. . . That the negro Babo was the one who plotted everything from first to last. He ordered every murder. He was, as it were, the helm and keel of the revolt.

. . . That Atufal was his lieutenant in everything. But Atufal committed no murder with his own hand. Neither did the negro Babo.

. . . That Atufal was shot and killed in the fight with the boats before the men boarded.

. . . That the adult negresses knew of the plan to revolt and declared that they were pleased at the death of their master, Don Alexandro.

. . . That they wanted to torture the Spaniards to death instead of just killing them as the negro Babo commanded. But the negroes restrained them.

. . . That the negresses used their utmost influence to have the witness done away with.

. . . That in the various acts of murder they sang songs and danced — not gaily but solemnly. And before the battle with the boats, as well as during the fighting, they sang melancholy songs to the negroes. The sad tone of these songs inflamed the negroes more than any other would have done, and was meant to.

. . . That all this is believed because the negroes have said it.

. . . That all the passengers are now dead.

. . . That of the thirty-six men of the crew which the witness had knowledge of, only six remain alive, together with four cabin-boys and ship-boys who are not included with the crew.

. . . That the negroes broke an arm of one of the cabin-boys and cut him with hatchets.

[*Then come various disclosures made at random referring to various periods of time. The following are extracted:*]

. . . That while Captain Amasa Delano was on board, some attempts were made by sailors and one by Hermenegildo Gandix to convey hints to him of the true state of affairs. But these attempts were unsuccessful. This was because the Spaniards feared being killed and because of the devices the negro Babo had worked out which gave a false impression of what was really going on. It was also because of the generosity and piety of Amasa Delano who was incapable of believing that such evil could exist.

... That Luys Galgo, a sailor about thirty years of age who had formerly served with the King's navy, was one of those who tried to convey hints to Captain Amasa Delano. But his intention was suspected, though not actually discovered. He was made to withdraw, and was eventually taken into the hold where he was killed. This the negroes have since said.

... That one of the ship-boys, feeling from Captain Amasa Delano's presence that there was a chance of rescue, dropped a hint to this effect. He didn't have enough sense to keep quiet. His words were overheard and understood by a slave-boy with whom he was eating at the time. The slave-boy struck the ship-boy over the head with a knife, inflicting a bad wound from which the boy is now recovering.

... That, similarly, not long before the ship was brought to anchor, one of the seamen, who was steering at the time, put himself in danger from an expression on his face that the blacks noticed which arose from the same feelings of hope that the ship-boy had had. But this sailor, by being prudent about his behaviour afterwards, escaped.

... That those statements are made to show the court that from the beginning to the end of the revolt, it was impossible for the witness and his men to act otherwise than they did.

... That the third clerk, Hermenegildo Gandix, had been forced to live among the seamen, wearing seamen's clothes and in all respects appearing to be one for the time. He was killed by a musket ball fired by mistake from the boats before landing. In his terror, he had run up the mizzen-rigging and called to the boats, 'Don't board', because he was afraid that if they did so, the negroes would kill him. This led the Americans to believe that he supported the negroes in some way. They fired two balls at him. He fell wounded from the rigging and was drowned in the sea.

... That the young Don Joaquin, Marques de Aramboalaza, like Hermenegildo Gandix, the third clerk, was degraded to the position and appearance of a common seaman.

... That on one occasion, when Don Joaquin flinched at something the negroes did, the negro Babo commanded the Ashanti Lecbe to take tar and heat it and pour it on Don Joaquin's hands.

... That Don Joaquin was killed owing to another mistake of the Americans, but one that they could not be blamed for. When the boats approached, the negroes made Don Joaquin appear on the bulwarks with a hatchet tied edge out and upright in his hand. Seen like this, with a weapon in his hand and in a questionable attitude, he was shot as a sailor who had joined the cause of the negroes.

... That on Don Joaquin's body was found a jewel. Documents that were found proved that this jewel was meant for the shrine of Our Lady of Mercy in Lima. It had been pledged as an offering for the safe conclusion of his voyage from Spain when he landed in Peru, his last destination.

... That the jewel, with the other effects of the late Don Joaquin, is in the custody of the brothers of the Hospital de Sacerdotes, awaiting the decision of the court.

... That the Americans were not forewarned that a passenger and one of the clerks had been disguised by the negro Babo as apparent members of the crew. This was because the witness was not in a fit state to inform them, and because the boats set out to attack the *San Dominick* with such haste.

... That as well as the negroes killed in the action, some were killed after the capture of the ship and she had been re-anchored for the night. This was while the negroes were shackled to the ring-bolts on deck. These deaths were committed by the sailors before they could be prevented.

... That as soon as he was informed of what was happening, Captain Amasa Delano used all his authority to stop it. In particular, with his own arm, he struck down Martinez Gola. He had found a razor in the pocket of an old jacket of his which one of the shackled negroes was wearing and was aiming it at the negro's throat.

. . . That the noble Captain Amasa Delano wrenched the dagger from the hand of Bartholomew Barlo. He had hidden this dagger on his person at the time of the massacre of the whites and was about to stab a shackled negro with it — that negro who the same day, together with another negro, had thrown him to the deck and jumped upon him.

. . . That the witness is unable to give an account here of all the events that occurred during the long time that the ship was in the hands of the negro Babo. But that what he has said includes the most important things that he can remember at present. And it is the truth under the oath which he has taken.

This statement he confirmed and agreed to after hearing it read to him.

He said that he is twenty-nine years of age and broken in body and mind. That when he was finally dismissed by the court, he did not intend to return to Chile. Instead, he would return to the monastery on Mount Agonia outside the city. He signed his statement under oath and crossed himself. Then he departed as he came, in his litter, with the monk Infelez, to the Hospital de Sacerdotes.

BENITO CERENO

DOCTOR ROZAS

Chapter 14
The End of the Story

It is to be hoped that these extracts from Don Benito's statement have served as the key to unlock the complications which precede them. If so, then the *San Dominick*'s hull lies open today like a vault whose door has been flung back.

Up till now, this story has not described events in the order in which they took place. This was inevitable given the fact that the story began with Captain Delano's view of the strange ship. The history of what happened before has had to be filled in retrospectively and irregularly. This is true also of the following passages which conclude the story.

During the long mild voyage to Lima, there was a period, as already indicated, during which Don Benito recovered his health to some extent — or at least he regained his tranquillity to a certain degree. Before he once more relapsed into sickness, the two captains had many friendly conversations. The sincerity and frankness with which they spoke to each other was in marked contrast to their previous reserve.

Again and again, Don Benito repeated how hard it had been to play the part forced on him by Babo.

'Ah, my dear friend,' Don Benito said on one occasion, 'there were those times when you thought me morose and ungrateful. You even, as you now admit, half thought I was plotting your murder. But at these very times, my heart was frozen. I could not even look at you. My thoughts were on the danger hanging over you, my kind benefactor, both on my ship and on your own. And as God lives, Don Amasa, I do not know if I could have nerved myself to make that leap into your boat simply out of a desire for my own safety. I doubt whether I could have done it if it had not been for the thought of what would happen to you should you return to your ship not knowing the truth. You, my best friend, with all the other men on board, would have been stolen upon that night while you were in your hammocks, and would never have wakened again in this world. Just remember how you walked this deck, how you sat in this cabin. Every inch of ground under you was mined. It was like a honeycomb. And I could not drop the least hint or take the slightest step towards making the truth clear. If I had done so, death, violent death — yours as well as mine — would have been the result.'

'True, true,' cried Captain Delano, starting at the thought. 'You have saved my life, Don Benito, more than I saved yours. You saved it too without my knowledge or assistance.'

'No, my friend,' returned Don Benito, courteous to the point of making a religion of it. 'You saved my life, but your life was protected by God. Just think of some of the things you did — all that smiling and chatting, that rash pointing and gesticulating. They killed my mate, Raneds, for less than these. But you had a safe-conduct from the Prince of Heaven through all dangers.'

'Yes, I know I owe everything to Providence. But I was feeling in a particularly good mood that morning. And to this were added compassion and charity at the sight of so much suffering — more apparent than real as it turned out. If I had felt differently, it is possible that some of my words and actions might have ended unhappily enough, as you suggest. Besides, those feelings I spoke of enabled me to get the better of momentary distrust. Just as well. If I had been more perceptive, it might have cost me my life without saving another's. Only at the end did my suspicions get the better of me, and you know how wide of the mark they then proved.'

'Wide indeed,' said Don Benito sadly. 'You were with me all day. You stood with me, sat with me, talked with me, looked at me, ate with me, drank with me. And yet, at the last, you took me for a monster, yet I was not only innocent, but the most pitiable of all men. Such is the power of evil intrigue and deception. Even the best man can make a mistake when judging the conduct of someone with whose situation he is unacquainted. But you were forced to it, and in time you realized your mistake. I wish that that could always be the case.'

'You generalize, Don Benito. And you grow mournful. The past is finished with. Why brood on it? Forget it. See, the bright sun there has forgotten it all, and the blue sea, and the blue sky. These have turned over new leaves.'

'Because they have no memory,' Don Benito replied dejectedly. 'Because they are not human.'

'But these mild trade winds that now fan your cheek, don't they come with a human-like healing to you? The trade winds are like warm friends, steadfast friends.'

'They may be steadfast,' Don Benito returned with a note of foreboding, 'but they waft me only to my tomb, Señor.'

'But you are saved,' cried Captain Delano, more and more astonished and pained. 'You are saved. What has cast such a shadow on you?'

'The African.'

There was silence. The moody man sat, slowly and unconsciously gathering his cloak about him as if it were a pall.

There was no more conversation that day.

But if Don Benito's melancholy sometimes made him grow silent on subjects such as that just described, there were others about which he never spoke at all. On these, all his old reserve descended again.

Ignoring the worst, and just to make things clear, one or two of them are here explained. The clothes, so precise and costly, which he had worn on the day on which these events took place, had not been willingly put on. And that silver-mounted sword, which seemed to be the symbol of despotic command, was not in fact a sword at all, but merely the ghost of one. The scabbard, artificially stiffened, was empty.

And what about the African whose brain, not body, had plotted and led the revolt? His slight frame, inadequate for what it held, immediately yielded to the superior muscular strength of his captor in the boat. When he saw that his plan was defeated, he uttered no sound and could not be forced to do so. His expression seemed to say, 'Since I cannot do deeds, I will not speak words.' He was put in irons in the hold with the rest and carried to Lima.

During the voyage, Don Benito did not visit him. He would not look at him, then or at any time later. He even refused to do so in court. When pressed by the judges, he fainted. It was on the testimony of the sailors alone that the legal identity of Babo rested.

Some months later, the African was executed — still without speaking. He was dragged to the gallows behind a mule. The body was burned to ashes. But for many days, the head — that hive of subtlety — was fixed on a pole in the Plaza. There it met the gaze of the citizens, unashamed.

And across the Plaza, the head looked towards St Bartholomew's Church in whose vaults slept then, as now, the recovered bones of Aranda.

And across the Rimac Bridge, the head looked towards the monastery on Mount Agonia outside the city. There, three months after being dismissed by the court, Benito Cereno, carried on his bier, did indeed follow his leader.

Afterword

I still have some doubts about whether I have done the right thing in retelling Herman Melville's story the way I have done. But then, if you have read this far, perhaps it is all right.

Melville wrote his story in 1855, and some of the words he used have changed their meanings or seem old-fashioned to us now. He used language in a much more formal way than most writers would today. His sentences tend to be very long, full of descriptive phrases and qualifications. This is appropriate in a story where mysteries are examined and puzzled over. But for many readers sentences like these can be exhausting and can deter them from reading on. Here is an example:

> With no small interest, Captain Delano continued to watch her — a proceeding not much facilitated by the vapours partly mantling the hull, through which the far matin light from her cabin streamed equivocally enough; much like the sun — by this time hemisphered on the rim of the horizon, and, apparently, in company with the strange ship entering the harbour — which, wimpled by the same low, creeping clouds, showed not unlike a Lima

intriguante's one sinister eye peering across the Plaza from the Indian top-hole of the dusk *saya-y-manta*.

What I have tried to do is rewrite the story in a language and style that today's reader would find more readily approachable. I have changed some of Melville's vocabulary, choosing words that are simpler or more immediately understandable today. I have broken up his long sentences into shorter more straightforward statements. I have used dialogue in some cases where Melville reported what was said. I have also added the chapter headings and changed the title — I don't think that many people, seeing *Benito Cereno* on the cover of a book, would feel an overwhelming urge to pick it up and read it.

But I have kept the tone reasonably formal. Slang and the more easy-going language of today would not sound right for a story taking place in 1799. And I have followed exactly every detail, idea and comparison of Melville's account. I have added nothing and omitted nothing. My version is simply 'a translation', as it were, from one language to another.

Now, some people will feel that this is not a proper thing to do. After all, Melville was a great writer, and the way a story is told is an important part of the story itself. Inevitably, something will be lost. Translations from foreign languages can never fully capture the flavour of the original. Modern versions of Shakespeare and the Bible are feeble compared with the richness of what Shakespeare wrote and of the Authorized Version. Stage, film and television adaptations of books usually lose something in the process.

So why do it? The answer is — hopefully — to bring the story to the attention of more readers. As suggested in the Foreword, Herman Melville's writing is virtually unread today. *Moby Dick* is one of the 'great unread classics', like *Don Quixote*. It is probably better known in its 'translated' form — the film by John Huston starring Gregory Peck, or in its stage version by Orson Welles. Similarly, Herman

Melville's *Billy Budd* is better known as a film or as an opera by Benjamin Britten.

I suspect that hardly anyone has even heard of *Benito Cereno*, though the American poet Robert Lowell has written a stage version — another 'translation'. And I want people to know about it and read it.

What I particularly want to bring to the attention of readers is the subject matter and the view it presents of racism. Captain Delano is a good-natured and compassionate man. He likes black people and feels friendly towards them. But when it comes down to it, his attitude is just as racist as that of the majority of white people of his day.

He patronises them. He sees them as simple creatures, affectionate and cheerful. They like bright colours. They make good body servants — natural valets and hairdressers. They are like pets, loyal and pleasant to joke with and to have around.

But above all, there is no doubt in Delano's mind that black people are morally and intellectually inferior to white people. This racist 'white supremacy' view is revealed again and again. For instance, he feels sure that in the case of the mulatto Francesco the mixture of a little white blood with black blood must be an improvement. He can't imagine any white man being such a traitor to his race as to join Africans in an evil scheme. Besides, black people are too stupid. They don't have the intelligence to plot and plan and deceive and defeat white people.

It is because of this racist attitude that Captain Delano is tricked and fails to see what is really happening on board the *San Dominick*. That is the whole irony of the story. Captain Delano, who considers himself as a member of the 'superior race', shows himself to be singularly lacking in perception. It is Babo who is the intelligent one. He is the one who uses his brain to work out the details of the plot and has the skill to carry it out. And at the end of the story, Babo's head, 'that hive of subtlety', stares out and meets unashamed the gaze of the white men he has tricked and so nearly defeated.

Of course, the things Babo does are horrifying. But then, he was a slave. Violence had been done to him in the first place. He had been captured, sold and transported from his native Senegal. He was someone else's property. That might not excuse what he did, but it explains it.

In some ways, Babo can be compared with Shakespeare's Macbeth who also committed murder, though in his case it was because of his ambition for power. In other circumstances, both men might have used their intellectual abilities for good, not evil. It was not just white people who were tainted and corrupted by slavery.

The horrors of slavery are not stressed in the story, but it is important to bear them in mind as a background to the events. A comment by the black American writer Toni Morrison may help to give you an impression of what slavery was like. She described it as 'like the Second World War going on for two hundred years'. It is difficult to support the view that violence can ever be justified. But in these circumstances, was there any alternative?

What Melville does show is that the violence was not one-sided. The assault by the American sailors on the *San Dominick* is brutal, spurred on by the motive of sharing in the spoils. Some of the Spanish sailors try to kill the defenceless shackled slaves in revenge.

As I have suggested, an extra dimension is given to Melville's story by the fact that it is based on real events. There was a Captain Amasa Delano who published a book entitled *A Narrative of Voyages and Travels in the Northern and Southern Hemispheres* in 1817. In that book he describes his sea-going experiences, including the events on board the *San Dominick*. Melville used the story exactly as set down by the real Captain Delano. He expanded it and added a few details of his own, but essentially it is Captain Delano's story. He even copied actual phrases from the captain's account, and more than half of the extracts given of Don Benito's statement come directly from official documents of the trial.

Since Melville got his ideas — and even some of his words — from another author, it could be seen as another justification for my 'translation'. But more important is the fact that it shows that slave revolts did occur. Slaves did not sit and passively endure the suffering that was imposed upon them. It is worth remembering that in 1799, the year of Babo's uprising, Toussaint L'Ouverture was consolidating his power in the black state of Haiti and extending it across the whole of Hispaniola.

Herman Melville himself was a remarkable person. He was born in New York City in 1819. He had a happy and comfortable childhood until his father went bankrupt in 1830, later dying insane. Melville worked at various jobs in New York and Massachusetts to make ends meet, but in 1839 he suddenly signed on as a cabin-boy. He experienced the squalor of life at sea at the time and travelled extensively to places as far apart as Liverpool and Tahiti. He was even imprisoned for his part in a mutiny.

These experiences helped to shape his character and formed the basis for much of his writing. His genius was not recognised in his lifetime, and he died in 1891 virtually unnoticed. It is only in the last fifty years that he has come to be regarded as one of the first great American writers.

Benito Cereno was written in 1855, five years before the American Civil War in which the North fought the South over the issue, among others, of slavery. The Captain Delano of the story came from Massachusetts. No doubt, he would have supported the North in their fight to free the slaves, but he would still have been a racist. What Herman Melville shows in *Benito Cereno* is how deep-seated racism is. It is not something that exists only in evil people. You can be kind and generous and compassionate, and still have racism hidden in your heart without even knowing it is there.

What Herman Melville said in 1855 is just as true today. Perhaps that is the real reason why I wanted you to know about and read this story.

Titles in the Adlib Series

Terry Edge
Fanfare For a Teenage Warrior in Love
In two and a half extraordinary weeks at Hornford Comprehensive Tom Hall falls in love, becomes a T.V. 'personality', gets caught up in a school betting shop, plays championship football — and survives with flying colours.   0 233 98080 6

Double-Crossing Duo
Further adventures of Tom Hall and Taff now two years older and living in Wales, but still full of schemes and ideas.   0 233 98319 8

Will Gatti
Berry Moon
An old family feud explodes into violence in the west of Ireland.   0 233 97828 3

Dennis Hamley
The Fourth Plane at the Flypast
A tragedy from the Second World War reaches out to affect the lives of Sue and John and their family.   0 233 97788 0

Haunted United
A ghostly footballer stalks the grounds of Bowland United.
0 233 97942 5

The Shirt Off a Hanged Man's Back
Nine spine-chilling tales of the supernatural.   0 233 97650 7

Charles Hannam
A Boy in Your Situation
A remarkable autobiography which follows the experiences of a young Jewish boy who flees to England as a refugee from Nazi Germany.   0 233 98279 5

Michael Hardcastle
No Defence
Where does a brilliant, young footballer go for his kicks?
0 233 97912 3

Minfong Ho
Rice Without Rain
Famine in a Thai village make an insecure background for Ned and Jinda's uneasy romance.   0 233 97911 5

Rhodri Jones
Slaves and Captains
A version of Herman Melville's *Benito Cereno*, the true story of an 18th century slave ship and the strange events that occur on it.
0 233 98356 2

Different Friends
It was learning the truth about Azhar that shocked Chris into changing his attitude to love, making him think for the first time what the word really meant.   0 233 98096 2

Getting It Wrong
If you're young and black, it is very easy to 'get it wrong' as Clive and Donovan find out.   0 233 97910 7

Hillsden Riots
What happens when the frustrations of young black people become intolerable.   0 233 97827 5

Pete Johnson
Catch You On the Flip Side
A sharp, lighthearted look at what happens to a boy, accustomed to girls falling for him, when he falls in love himself.
0 233 98074 1

Secrets from the School Underground
To find out what's really going on at Farndale Comprehensive you have to 'read' the writing on the wall behind the bike shed — a sort of unofficial school newspaper.   0 233 97987 5

Geraldine Kaye
Great Comfort
Comfort Kwatey Jones is half British and half Ghanaian. She loves being in Ghana, but when she goes to stay with her grandmother there, she discovers that she does not know the country and its traditions as well as she imagines.   0 233 98300 7

A Breath Of Fresh Air
Amy's interest in a school project on slavery becomes a reality when she slips back in time to experience life as a black slave in eighteenth century Jamaica.   0 233 98163 2

John Kirkbride
In Reply to Your Advertisement
Kevin Daughtry may not have a job but he is a persistent and imaginative letter writer and through his application letters and the replies he receives we get to know him more and like him better.   0 233 98344 9

Elisabeth Mace
Under Siege
The fantasy world of a sophisticated board game becomes an obsession with Morris Nelson and the characters involved in the game more important than the people around him.
0 233 98345 7

Beware the Edge
The perils of dabbling in the supernatural.   0 233 97908 5

Boxes
Rona Goodall is an old maid of eighteen and desperate for a boyfriend. Along comes Sean and her problems seem to be solved.   0 233 97670 1

Suzanne Newton
I Will Call It Georgie's Blues
Bitter family tension threatens the youngest son of a preacher in the American Deep South.   0 233 97720 1

Eduardo Quiroga
On Foreign Ground
A young Argentinian soldier in the Falklands remembers his love
affair with an English girl.   0 233 97909 3

Caryl Rivers
Virgins
A bitter-sweet story of American high school girls growing up in
the fifties.   0 233 97791 0

Margaret Simpson
The Drug Smugglers
Paul decides to track down the drug pushers who are supplying his
sister.   0 233 97673 6

Andy Tricker
Accidents Will Happen
The author's own moving account of a motorbike accident which
left him paralysed, and his struggle to regain a measure of
independence.   0 233 98095 4

Rosemary Wells
The Man in the Woods
Is he an ordinary hooligan or a more sinister figure mysteriously
connected with events of the American Civil War of a hundred
years ago?   0 233 97785 6

When No One Was Looking
Young American tennis star, Kathy Bardy, resents her new rival
but she didn't expect her to die.   0 233 97669 8